# finding
## *nathan*

# finding

## *nathan*

# HJ Harley

Edited by Murphy Rae of Indie Solutions
Cover Design by Sommer Stein of Perfect Pear Creative
Interior Formatted by Tianne Samson with E.M. Tippetts Book Designs
emtippettsbookdesigns.com

# books by
## H.J. Harley

**Love Lies Bleeding Series**
*Finding Jordie*
*Finding Nathan*
*Finding Rachel* (Coming Soon)

**Love and Sacrafice Series**
*Hit or Mistletoe*

*For Carrie Papandrea Devivi*

*I'm sorry I didn't get this finished in time for you to read it. Rest easy my friend. You put up one hell of a fight. CANCER SUCKS.*

# prologue

I WADDLED MY ASS to the couch and leaned back slowly to take a seat next to Fiona. Once I was down, I propped my feet up on the ottoman and let out a huge sigh, trying to catch my breath.

"You need anything, sweetheart?" Fiona asked as she rubbed my gigantic belly.

"I need him out. That's what I need. Do you hear me in there?" I shouted playfully at my stomach. Nate Jr. already had one of my worst habits: being late for everything. Which included being born. He was officially four days late. Nathan and I had tried *everything*—from what the books and Internet said, like have sex or walk a lot, and even what Navi the Falafel guy had suggested to help induce labor. Which pretty much consisted of eating jasmine rice and cleaning the house. Keeps you busy and moving around. Nothing worked. This baby was stubborn like me too, apparently.

"We can't wait to meet you, little man." Fiona leaned over and spoke right next to my stomach. I flipped the TV on and got as comfortable as possible.

"What time is it? They should be arriving about now." I put on the E!

Channel.

Nathan had an event at the Metropolitan Museum of Art and I was in no shape to go, so he took Emma. Luckily I had tuned in just a few minutes before they walked the red carpet.

"Do you want me to fix you something to eat? You're looking pale, Jordan," Fiona said in a worried, motherly tone.

"Ma, I'm fine. Thank you though." I had finally stopped moving around for a few minutes when a pain shot right through me and I shifted awkwardly to get up.

"What? What is it?" Fiona sprang to her feet.

"Just a sharp pain. It's gone." I had my hands on my waist towards my back for support.

"I'll call Frank." She scurried for her phone.

"No, no, I'm good. Probably just gas," I assured her. She clutched her phone in her hand for dear life.

"Are you sure, Jordan?" She was the pale one now.

"I'm fine. Really. I'll just walk around a bit, get it moving." I smiled and began to pace.

After a few couples walked the red carpet, I caught sight of Nathan and Emma in the background posing for pictures. Emma fidgeted a bit and blinked a lot. I guessed the camera flashes were bothering her eyes.

Frank ushered Nathan and Emma towards their spot in front of the camera. There they stood, my beautiful daughter and gorgeous husband. Above the noise of the screaming fans, a woman's voice could be heard. "I love you, Nate!" she screeched, and Fiona and I busted out laughing when Emma rolled her eyes on live television.

*Oh, ouch. Ouch. Ouchhhh.*

"Ohhh my god. Holy shiiiiit!" I screamed, doubled over and held my breath to try and control the pain.

"Nope, not gas. Contraction. Call Frank," I said as I exhaled. Now, I know they say you forget the pain of childbirth but let me make myself very clear when I say it's like riding a bike. As soon as you hop on that shit it all comes back to you, and holy crap was it coming back to me. I stood up and took a few deep breaths. Fiona dialed and began doing breathing exercises with me.

"In and out, in and out," she repeated over and over.

I saw Frank look at his phone on the TV and answer it.

"It's time, Frank. She's in labor," she yelled in both fear and excitement. I heard Frank interrupt the live interview, telling Nathan I was in labor. Emma was the first to take off, with Frank and Nathan close behind. The interviewer congratulated us and then another wave of pain crashed over me. This time, though, I felt a huge amount of pressure between my legs and then—almost immediately—it was gone. *My water broke.*

"Frank, her water just broke. I'm getting her ready now. Is there a car downstairs?" Fiona asked as she grabbed my coat and overnight bag out of the closet.

"Charles is coming around the corner; I just sent him a message. We will meet you there," Frank said. I heard Nathan ask for the phone as I wiggled out of my now soaking wet yoga pants and into the sweats I had in my bag.

"Baby, how you feeling?" Nathan came through the speaker.

"Like a peach, Nathan," I said through clenched teeth, trying to concentrate on my breathing. I went to put my jacket on, but another contraction stopped me in my tracks and I screamed.

"These are coming too fast." I panted as we headed to the door. Fiona draped my jacket over my shoulders and, halfway down the stairs, Charles came in and helped me the rest of the way to the car. Fiona locked up and we were out.

"Jordie, I'm almost there. I'll meet you at the entrance. I love you. I love you so much, baby." He sounded choked up.

"I love you too. Call Rachel, please. She'll make me stuff this kid back in and do it all over if she isn't there for it," I said between breaths.

"I already did, Mom," I heard Emma say.

"Thanks. I love you guys," I said before I let out another scream. Thank the good lord we weren't too far from the hospital because this kid was ready to meet us.

# chapter *one*

GOING TO THE DMV was never on my list of top ten favorite things to do. Going to the DMV sleep-deprived, cranky, and smelling like spit-up made it that much *more* pleasurable. Nathan and I got married on New Year's Eve, but I was too pregnant to deal with the shenanigans of the Division of Motor Vehicles. After that I was simply procrastinating, but my license was about to expire so I had to go.

"Harper? Jordan Marie Harper?"

I barely heard my name through my dream-like state, as I sat straight up in what may have been the least comfortable chair my ass had ever felt.

"Jordie?" Rachel nudged me. "Wake up and go get your shit. Give me Nate."

She reached over and took my little man from my arms.

I wiped the corner of my mouth as I walked up to the counter to get the first glimpse of my new mug shot. I felt like canned ass. It had been a long ten years between kids and I was definitely out of practice.

I shuffled my feet back to the entrance where Rachel was waiting. She snatched the license out of my hand to admire the new credentials.

"Ooh, this is rich. You look like death had you for breakfast," she snorted.

"Eff off," I quipped with no effort and a small smile as we walked out to my truck. "I need a nap."

"I hath no pity on thee. You're the one who refuses the help. Seriously, it's like Nathan isn't *allowed* to be a father at times." She reached for her seatbelt as I started the truck.

"Rachel, he works all day, and sometimes half the night. I can't ask him to stay up all night with him."

"You aren't asking him. He volunteers. You just take away his man card and tell him no. Besides, it isn't like he's out there working at the quarry busting his ass all damn day." She rolled her eyes.

"The quarry?" I snorted amusedly as I pulled out of the parking lot.

"When will you learn you can't and don't have to do this alone? You're married. Capiche?"

"Exactly, and I'm trying to be the best wife possible. There are a million chicks who wish they could be me and I don't want to give him a reason to replace me." My voice cracked a bit.

"Yeah, okay, you hormonal nightmare. Like Nathan sees any other woman than you? Please, you're a dumbass for even saying that. You *know* how much he loves you," she said as she put on a fresh coat of lip gloss.

Just as we pulled up to my place, Nathan Jr. fell asleep. I was so thankful, because that meant I could take an almost three-hour nap before Emma got home from school. I hugged Rachel goodbye before she headed out, and my text alert went off as I walked to the front of the bar. I put Nate down in his carseat carrier and pulled out my phone.

Nathan: Tomorrow is still good for you, right?

*Shit. Slipped my mind.*

Me: Yepp.

I forgot we had an appointment with the realtor. How could I forget something like that? Especially since my apart—*our* apartment—had turned into a sardine can overnight. Between what Nathan had moved in and all the baby's new stuff, it felt like ten pounds of shit crammed into a five-pound bag in there.

As if that weren't reason enough to move, things were getting a bit ridiculous with the paparazzi; they had set up shop on the curb out front. Then there were the daily deliveries of gifts for Nathan. I understood how grateful Nathan was for his fans but it had gotten out of control. Without Isobel and Todd giving the paps info, it'd become a free-for-all. It got so bad that Frank had to move in downstairs, which I didn't mind at all.

There were many reasons to move but only one to stay: my bar. It wasn't much, but it was mine. Yeah, Nathan had money and I was his wife but that didn't make his money mine. Well, it made it mine by default but not definition. Whereas the bar was mine, business was great and I saw no reason to sell it. Compromising, we decided on the Upper East Side of Manhattan to allow me to be close to the bar—plus, security was tighter which would give Frank a bit of a break. Emma's routine wouldn't change much, and Central Park was within walking distance. All right, there were a ton of positives in moving there. I was just thankful Nathan compromised so well.

Nathan: It's a date. Love you.

Me: Love you too.

I smiled. He always knew how to make me do that, no matter what my mood was. And I'll admit my mood had been all over the place since I had the baby. My hormones were so out of whack. Nathan regained his memory about three weeks before Nate was born, so we got married in a quick ceremony on the rooftop and he moved in. Everything changed with lightning speed once again. After spending seven months without him, pregnant and broken-hearted, I had to readjust to him being there. It was an adjustment I was more than happy to make. I was whole again. Not that I fell apart at the seams while Nathan was—um, what should I call it—recovering? I didn't lock myself in a room wasting away in my own filth and crying for months on end—nothing like that. Life went on, but at a slower pace. Partly because I was pregnant as hell and I couldn't move any faster, but mainly because my heart was so heavy.

When Nathan walked into the apartment twenty-three minutes later, I handed Nate over, kissed them both, picked up the bagel and coffee brought home for me and headed upstairs.

"I love you but I'm so tired," I dragged my tired body upstairs, dodging a pile of laundry, a baby swing and two huge boxes of diapers. I felt like the luckiest woman in the world.

When I woke up, Nathan's mom was there. She had come over to spend some time with the baby. Plus, I was pretty sure she knew I was a chicken-shit when it came to staying home alone. Nathan had to be at a meeting downtown so he made sure she was there to babysit me. I guess subconsciously I still wasn't over what happened with Jason and all that mess. When I got down there, she was folding the towels.

"Mom, you don't have to do that. I'll get it. Here, take the baby. He wants his GiGi." I smiled and stood next to her.

After Nathan and I got married, I once made the mistake of calling his mother by her first name, Fiona. She hugged me and said, "None of that, Jordie. I'm Mom now." I just stood there frozen with my arms at my side, stiff as a shot of Wild Turkey. I thought about how long it had been since I'd last said that word. When I snapped out of it a few seconds later, I hugged her back. "All right…Mom." It must've been obvious I was trying the word on for size, because Fiona laughed, drew back, and took my face in her hands. "Well, that was convincing." She kissed my forehead. "You'll adjust."

By now, I was used to calling her Mom.

"Oh, hush your face. You know I don't mind. You have so much going on here. This is the least I can do to help out." She said the last half of the sentence in a baby-talk voice as she took Nate out of my arms and smiled at her grandson.

"Thank you. I appreciate it." I gave her a kiss on the cheek. "Mind if I hop in the shower?" I picked up two unfolded towels and laughed because it was as if I were no longer in the room. She was too busy making faces and playing with Nate to even hear me.

I turned the water on full blast—hot as I could take it, threw my clothes in a rumpled pile on the floor, and got in. I washed up quickly, shaved my legs, then stood there and savored every last drop of the steamy goodness as it washed over me. After I dried my hair, I plopped on our bed and opened up my laptop. I needed to order some stuff online. Primarily some nighttime attire because any time I went out, the paparazzi never failed to get pics of what I was buying. I know we're a public family now but I didn't particularly want the world knowing what I wore to bed for my husband. While perusing the web I saw a sponsored ad with Nathan's face on a pillowcase.

"Oh, look. Free shipping on all items." I laughed to myself and clicked on the link. I found the fuzzy slippers with his name on them cute, but the underwear and sweatpants that had 'Mrs. Harper' written across the ass completely wigged me out. I clicked on the underwear link.

"One thousand in stock? How much are these mofos? What. The. Fuck. *I'm* Mrs. Harper."

I felt my face getting hot. I mean, okay, I *knew* women—all kinds of women, hundreds of thousands of women of all ages—*loved* Nate Harper. I got that a long time ago. I was fine with it because I knew Nathan loved me. Not only me but our family, too. We were an actual family. When he walked through the doors, he was no longer Nate. He was Nathan or Daddy.

I heard Nathan come home. He talked to his mom for a few minutes, then came upstairs to the bedroom. I noticed how tired he looked as he took off his tie and hung it over the doorknob, then toed off his shoes.

"Hey, baby," he said after the second shoe was off, and walked over to the bed.

"Hey, handsome. How'd it go?"

"Great, actually. I'm excited about this project. I'm a bit nervous about being behind the camera, but more excited than anything. How was your night? Feeling okay?" He sat on the edge of the bed and lay back, exhaling loudly.

"Yep, everything's fine. Did a bit of shopping," I smiled and tapped my laptop.

"I knew you'd love the Internet once I showed you the world of shopping. What did you buy?" He tied the string on his shorts.

"Just some lingerie." I smiled mischievously.

"For me?" He wiggled his eyebrows.

"Of course." I leaned over and kissed him.

There was a knock at the door and I pulled back.

"Come in," Nathan answered.

"Goodnight," Emma said as she yawned and hugged Nathan first, then gave me a hug and a kiss.

Fiona walked in with a sleeping Nate in her arms and handed him to Nathan.

"I just called a cab," she whispered.

"Ma, no. Frank can take you home. Or I can, just give me two minutes to get dressed," Nathan said in a hushed voice, standing up.

"No, it's fine. I like the cab ride home. It's something new every time," Fiona said, kissing Nathan on the cheek, then Emma.

"I will see you Thursday, sweetheart." She leaned over and gave me a kiss on the top of my head before I could get out of bed.

"Yep." I said, standing up to give her a hug.

"Thank you again for tonight." I pulled back.

"Stop thanking me. We're family." She smushed my cheeks together.

"GiGi, will you tuck me in before you leave?" Emma asked Fiona.

"Already planned on it." Fiona put her arm around Emma and they walked out of the room.

"I'll go put him down and lock up," Nathan said, still holding our sleeping son, then leaned over to kiss me.

# chapter *two*

THE SMOOTH ELEVATOR RIDE and nearly angelic ding that followed as we reached the 33rd floor reminded me of where we were—on the West Side of Manhattan, Trump Place, Riverside Drive. *On the West Side.* Of course, there were plenty of apartments and penthouses available on the East Side, but there was no way on God's green earth we were spending that sort of money on a place smaller than mine.

We'd gone back and forth about that for a few days. I couldn't wrap my head around spending four-point-seven-mil on a two-thousand-square-foot apartment. Not to mention, the thought of not having that little "E." in my address bugged me. A lot. I loved the East Village. Period. It'd always been the down-to-earth, fun and trendy side of the island. Once you crossed over 42nd Street it was all suits and ties, business and Berkins. I *so* didn't want a Berkin. The reality of it, though, was I could afford a Berkin. My life had changed so drastically from the previous year I pretty much had to live in a swank tank like that.

Nathan put his hand on the small of my back for me to get out of the elevator first. My reflection greeted me in the smoky-colored mirrored hallway. There were two apartments on the floor. Our Real Estate agent, Gabby, turned to the left and the annoying-as-hell clickity-clack of her high heels led the way. Rachel's heels never sounded like that. Then again, Rachel never walked on Italian marble in an empty hallway…well, maybe she did when she went to Rome, but that didn't count. I didn't hear it. Once I walked past noisy-heel girl, I tuned back in to what she was saying about this nearly eight-thousand-square-foot penthouse monstrosity at the bargain price of nine million.

The view was amazing, and we would have our own rooftop terrace. That's how most of them were on the East Side; this was the only one we'd found on the West, which I loved for obvious reasons. Because not having a private rooftop would definitely suck, but mainly for safety reasons. Nate could never get up there and I loved being able to go up and read or have a lazy night with Nathan in the bed-lounger swing he put up. By the time we hit the en-suite, you know, the room also known as a *big fucking bathroom*, I had seen enough. I was getting more and more pissed off at myself because I actually loved it. I felt like I was betraying my sardine can of an apartment somehow. Like once we moved out of it the reality would set in that this is my life now. I loved my life, but I wasn't ready to let go of my old one completely yet. Would I feel like I was losing a huge chunk of myself only to replace it with a bigger chunk? No matter what, the bigger chunk wouldn't be the same as the smaller one. And that scared the shit out of me.

"I need to go. Like, now." I turned on my heel and headed towards the door.

*Jeeeesus, this kitchen is gorgeous.*

Nathan was a good distance behind me, but I heard him thank Gabby for her time and we needed time to discuss it. When they reached me, I was staring at the elevator doors with my arms folded.

"You'd think for millions of dollars this place would come equipped with a decent elevator." I pushed the button again, repeatedly.

"Assaulting the button won't make it get here any faster, babe." Nathan held back a smile as he took my hand. Gabby let out a small noise that resembled Beaker from the Muppets, so I shot her a look.

"Oh no." She searched her pockets. "I forgot my phone inside. I need to get it and make sure everything is locked up anyhow. It was a pleasure seeing you both again." She gave me an almost nonexistent head nod before she addressed Nathan.

"If you have any questions or come to any decisions please don't hesitate to call me." She smiled and hurried on back into the apartment.

The elevator ride was silent. The car ride home was awkward. The two flights of steps to the door of our place finally broke the silence.

"You know, that slow elevator was way quicker than this." Nathan grinned as he held the door open for me.

I smirked back at him, dropped my bag on the table, and plopped on the couch.

Nathan walked past me and into the kitchen.

I let out a huge sigh as a stress reliever, sprawled out on the couch, and propped myself up on my elbows.

"What are we going to do? I mean, I see nothing wrong with the brownstone on East 26th street. You didn't like that?" I sort of whined and begged at the same time.

"Jordan, it's the same size as this, twice the price, and our front door would still be on the street. Again. C'mon, you know why we're moving. I can't understand for the life of me why you're being so difficult." Nathan came out of the kitchen holding a bottle of water and sat down next to me.

I sat up all the way and leaned my head on his shoulder.

"You're right, I'm wrong. I'm sorry. I like the penthouse on Park Avenue." I plucked a piece of lint off my shirt and looked at him. He had a shit-eating grin on his face.

"Say it again…" He chuckled.

"I like the penthouse on Park Avenue," I repeated.

"No, the part where you said I was right and you were—wait, what was that again? *Wrong?* Oh shit, someone please send the devil a parka because Hell just froze over," he teased.

"Oh, shut up."

I playfully shoved his shoulder and the next thing I knew he was on top of me, trying to grab my wrists. I tried to wriggle out and hold them above my head but I felt my back slide against the couch, and then we were on the floor. With his face buried in between my shoulder and neck, he began to kiss me.

He stopped suddenly and took my wrists in one hand while he propped himself up with the other. "What time will everyone be back?"

"Does it really matter at this point?"

I nudged my hips up with a small laugh. I could feel him against me.

"It just depends on whether I'm going to take you right here or we're stripping on the way upstairs."

He sat up, pulled his shirt over his head, and tossed it over his shoulder. He hovered over me with the grin that made my heart pound and girl parts tingle. *Yes, I said girl parts.*

"I don't need my mom walking in on us. Especially with my kids in tow." He pulled the hem of my shirt up and ran his hands down over my breasts.

I combed my hands through his hair as he took full advantage of my position. Finally, I found the air to ask what time it was.

"Unless you have a clock down here, I have no idea and I don't care anymore," he said while he kissed me and worked the button and zipper of my jeans.

"I don't have one, but I can see you do. What is that, Big Ben you got in there?" I chuckled as I slid my hand down the front of his pants.

"My wifey is witty, gorgeous, and willing? Shit, I hit the trifecta with you, baby," he teased me as he got on his knees and tugged off my boots and jeans.

I had no idea of the time, and, to be honest, I was beyond caring. I grabbed his belt and fumbled around with it until it was undone, then did the same with his jeans. These days, everything was so rushed and chaotic that we never really had the time to do the spontaneous hop-on-the-counter-and-do-me-right-now thing anymore. It was nice to have a shot at getting rugburned again or breaking something and not worrying about it until later.

He still made my body react in a way it never had before I met him. I got lost whenever he touched me. Something about that carefree moment changed me. I think that's the moment I snapped out of my perpetual state of Grumparella, because I had it all, and if I were anyone else on the outside looking in, I'd be calling myself a whiney selfish brat who had no idea how great her life was. The clothes came off more quickly and the breathing got heavier. By the third growl, he had me bent over the side of the couch, yanking on a fistful of my hair. *Jesus Christ, I missed this.* I pushed back against him and turned around to face him. Somehow, we went from standing to me being on top of him. Looks like I was getting that rug burn after all. Just as I was about to explode, we heard the downstairs door shut. Emma and Fiona were talking as they walked up the steps. I heard Rachel's muffled laugh.

"Holy shit!" Nathan said, then busted out laughing. He reached for his jeans with me still on top of him. I was trying to process what was happening because two seconds prior I was in a completely different zone.

"Oh my god!" I jumped up as Nathan winced, yanking his jeans up with no boxers to protect him.

"Here." He tossed me his shirt since I couldn't find mine.

We were both laughing as we tried to make it around all the shit in the hallway to get upstairs.

"I've made it my entire life so far without my mother ever walking in on me and here I am, twenty-eight years old, chafing myself on jeans and pulling my wife up the steps behind me like a teenager," he muttered.

I laughed.

As we made it to the top of the steps, I heard the door open and Emma's backpack hit the floor with a thud as Rachel huffed about something. Fiona asked Emma to close the door.

"Emma, go start your homework, sweetie. Your mom and Nathan must be napping," I heard Fiona say.

Thank God. Nathan and I needed a quick shower, and not a cold one either. I heard my text message alert go off in our bedroom so I went in to get it. It was a text from Rachel.

Rachel: Hey twat-muffin… Pick up yours and your famous husband's skivvies off the floor before you scurry upstairs half-neked. Or else I'll sell his on eBay next time. That's rent for like a year, ya know.

I busted out laughing and texted her back.

Me: Thanks, hooch. We'll be down in a few...lol. Hollerr.

Rachel: Yeah. OK. Sure you will. LOL. Make sure you ice that rug burn if I'm not here to remind you when you two get done. Hollerrrr <3

I grinned. Rachel knew me all too well.

We got in the shower and picked up right where we where we left off. We had to make it quick and that was when it was clear to me. It didn't matter if we took our time or rushed it, if we did it on the bed or on the floor. All that mattered was us. I loved the feel of him against me. I loved how I felt when he was close to me. I was thankful that never got old. We were comfortable enough with one another to have no insecurities or care about anything else but the moment. And what a fabulous moment it was. He gave a whole new meaning to 'nailed my ass to the wall,' that's for sure.

*Fuck. Yes.*

"Mrs. Harper, the things you do to me." He smirked.

All I could do was smile.

# chapter *three*

ONCE WE DECIDED ON a new place to live, everything seemed to go a lot more smoothly and a lot less stressfully. I *finally* hired a full staff at the bar so Rachel only had to go in at night to close up and pay the bills. I'd come to terms with the fact that I couldn't do it all. I had to let go of some things. While the bar was a huge part of me, it was a part I could live without; I couldn't live without Emma, Nathan, Nate, or Rachel, so I had to pick my battles. The bar it was. I mean, I still owned it; Rachel was just the head honcho now. Amber was still there. In fact, she'd beefed up those titties of hers with a boob job. They looked nice and felt surprisingly real.

*Don't ask.*

Rachel and I grilled about fifty applicants until we came up with the lucky number seven to hire. The Post now had ten employees and one owner. I was impressed. It was like a real grown-up place to work now. Complete with schedules and all. *Ugh. Now I have to make schedules?* So with the bar covered, I had plenty of time to focus on the move and my family.

Nathan was going to have to go to LA for a few weeks the next month, so we were trying desperately to get the closing on the penthouse done ASAP, that way he could be there for the move. And somehow, we managed to pull it off.

A company had come to pack up the entire apartment, but I didn't feel right about having some stranger handling our personals, so I did the stuff like clothing, pictures, and our laptops. There was some *very* sensitive security footage on Nathan's computer. Okay, well, it wasn't *exactly* security footage. It was more like good-cop-dirty-cop-in-the-bedroom type of footage. My husband always looked like a sexy man beast when he was on-screen. No matter what role he was playing. I didn't look too bad myself. Those videos, though—they would put Kim K and Paris Hilton out of business for good in the wrong hands. I was always up Nathan's ass about deleting them after we watched them. He needed to. I don't trust technology as much as the rest of the planet does. Up until last year I was still reading newspapers. He was more confident and would always assure me that nobody but he and I could access those files. They were up in the clouds or some techy bullshit like that. Eventually I grew tired of asking and just said *fuck it.* I had too many other things on my plate to be worried about trivial things.

It was a godsend that Nathan's parents moved to New York. A lot of my time was freed up. They would come and take Nate every morning, get themselves some coffee and a take stroll through a park. They alternated their spots and, in the few hours they had him, I worked my ass off. Usually for the first hour *Nathan* was working my ass off…off the counter…off the couch… off the rooftop. You get the point, I'm sure. I was so happy things were getting back to normal. I knew once we got moved and settled in it would be back to one-hundred-percent. No chaos, no tripping over stuff going upstairs, and no more paps camped out on our stoop. We were in the home stretch on the road to drama-free land.

Close to a week later, we closed and started the move.

"I'm going to miss this place," Emma said, hugging me around my waist.

"Are you now? I thought you hated the steps and all the noise at night. You going to miss that too?" I laughed as I kissed the top of her head.

She looked up at me with the most serious face I'd ever seen and she said to me, "This is the only place I've lived, Mom. What if I don't like the new place as much?"

She meant it. Whatever anxiety Emma was having about moving, it was real, and I had to help her move past it quickly.

"Em, we're not selling this place. I promise you, I'll keep this building until the day I die and then you'll get it. Shit, when you're ready to go out on your own, this will be here for you, baby." I tried to reassure her.

"Really? You'd let me live here when I turn eighteen?" Her eyes lit up and excitement rang through her voice.

"Well, I said when you're ready, not when you turn eighteen, and I promise to charge you half of the going rental prices." I nudged her.

"Ha ha ha, rent. Yeah, right. You wouldn't do that to me. Would you?" She looked up at me with uncertainty in her eyes.

"Yup, unless you're in college full time. Then you can live here rent-free. Deal?" I stuck out my pinky.

"Deal," she said, latching her pinky with mine.

Emma and Nathan took some personal stuff over to the new place, and I stayed behind while the last of our stuff was loaded on the truck. Plus, I needed to do a quick run-through to make sure everything was out, and shut off the main breaker either until I got it rented out or winter came.

I stood in the middle of the empty room and spun around slowly, checking out every corner, every mark on the wall, and every scuff on the floor. Each of them had a memory. I couldn't believe this was it. I never thought I'd ever see the day, yet here it was. There was one last stop on memory lane before I locked up and headed out. I ran upstairs, flung open the bedroom window, and headed to the rooftop. I stood against the wall and took in one last look at the gorgeous view. I realized I was standing in the exact spot where Nathan and I first kissed. Suddenly the thought entered my mind that maybe I wouldn't miss this place as much as I thought I would, because, truth be told, as long as I had my family, I could live anywhere.

Speaking of family, my sister, Kelly, was so excited we were moving to Park Avenue. She insisted they had the cutest doormen, cuter than on any other block. She was such a loon. When I walked over to the rooftop entrance door to make sure it was secured and locked, I noticed a pack of cigarettes sitting there. Nathan must have left them up here before he quit, which was only recently, so I picked up the pack of smokes and took them downstairs with me. I locked up the rest of the place and headed outside.

I sat on the front stoop and pulled out the cigarettes. It had a pack of matches inside the cellophane, so I figured, *Ah, what the hell. What's one for old times' sake?* I took out a smoke and struck the match to light it. I expected that first inhale to be heavenly. Holy shit, was I wrong. I coughed and completely ruined my obligatory, sentimental goodbye moment.

I stared at the lit stink-stick and let out a small laugh as I butted it out. Just then, Frank pulled up to the curb.

"Tsk tsk, young lady." He laughed.

"Well, shit, you caught me. I was trying to have a *Sex in the City* kind of moment. You know, saying goodbye all cool and calm with a smoke. A 'thanks for the memories, kid' type of deal." I laughed at Frank's expression. It was a cross between *what the fuck?* and *have you lost your shit?*

"Aw, c'mon. Cut me some slack. I'm really going to miss this place." I stood up and brushed off my butt. Frank mumbled something about things being all about me me me, but I let it go. He hadn't been his normal self for a few weeks now, and it was getting more and more evident something was wrong. He seemed preoccupied and distant. I wondered if everything was okay with his family. I made a mental note to catch him alone later to see what was up.

# chapter *four*

WHEN WE PULLED UP to the building—our new home—a young man opened the door for me. *That will take some getting used to.* I walked around to the trunk where Frank was getting out a box.

"Do I tip him every time he opens a door for me?" I whispered curiously.

"No, it's included in your building fees." Frank laughed and shut the trunk door.

When we walked into the new place, it was exciting and refreshing. I took a second and stood at the door with a smile.

"Admire it after you're all moved in and get your ass in here. Help me. I'm not doing this by myself, and you're a damn hoarder." I heard Rachel's voice come from somewhere behind the wall of boxes in the living area.

"Whatever, asshole," I yelled out to her and dropped myself by the door.

"Hello, gorgeous," I heard Nathan say as he walked down the hallway towards me, wearing my smile.

He wrapped his arms around me and kissed me like he hadn't seen me in a week.

"Holy hell, you two. Seriously?" Rachel scoffed as she attempted to get the tape off a box marked **MISCELLANEOUS**.

"I'm bound and determined to find my Michael Kors bag, you sticky-fingered bitch," she mumbled playfully.

"And here's one of them fingers just for you," I said to Rachel as I walked past her, flipping her off.

Nathan showed me around and I started to feel overwhelmed with happiness. I exhaled to try and calm myself.

"What's up?" Nathan asked as we were walking out of our bedroom towards Nate's room.

"Nothing is wrong. Everything is just right." I wiped my eyes before the tears that had welled up could fall.

"I love you. Look where we're standing. This is a second chance for both of us to be a part of something amazing. Us, our kids, my mom and dad, Tyler, and I guess even Rachel…" He nodded his head back and smiled.

"I heard that, asshole," Rachel yelled from the living room.

"Ah, damn, the baby monitor is on in here, isn't it?" He chuckled.

We both laughed and I stood up on my tippy toes to give him a kiss. "I don't know what I did to deserve you."

"If I had to guess, I'd probably say you endured life with that criminally insane ex-husband of yours."

"Ha ha. Very funny." I smacked his arm lightly as we headed back to the living room.

"What. The. *Fuck*? Jordan, seriously, bitch. You gone and lost your damn mind. What *is* all this?" Rachel said very loudly and slowly.

"What are you yelling about?" Frank asked all three of us as he walked over to stand by Rachel.

There it was, in all its glory—the box marked **PERSONAL, DO NOT TOUCH—ESPECIALLY YOU, RACHEL!**

The box just sat there, wide open, along with Rachel's mouth. She slowly raised her arms and turned to face us, holding a pair of white boy-short panties with **MRS. HARPER** slapped across the ass in bright red letters.

Nathan shrugged his shoulders.

"What's the big deal? She *is* Mrs. Harper." He paused. "Okay, yeah, what gives?" He looked confused.

Rachel tried to stifle her laugh because she knew what Nathan didn't.

"Oh, it's a big deal all right." She threw the panties at me and I busted out laughing.

"This. It's literally a big deal," Rachel confirmed, waving the packing slip around.

"What? Is it a crime for me to go lingerie-shopping?" I tried to take the packing slip from her and I widened my eyes to hint for her to shut the fuck up.

"Oh, Jesus, I can't stand when you two talk all cryptic. It's like a different frequency that only you two can hear." Nathan snagged the slip from Rachel's hands and scanned the invoice.

"Wow, I'd say at a dollar each you got the best deal ever, considering these things retail for about fifteen bucks a pop. And this was your lingerie-shopping?" He shook his head and smiled as he wrapped his arms around me and kissed my forehead.

I squinted at him. "I may or may not be disturbed by you knowing that."

Nathan's parents had made it back with the kids just as I was closing up the box. She informed us that he needed a diaper change because he made a "boom boom" on the cab ride home. Nathan's dad pointed out how it actually made the cab smell better. All I could do was laugh. He was such a quick-witted guy. Always wise-crackin'. I went to take Nate from Fiona but decided better of it and asked Nathan to do it. It may have only been a shitty diaper but we had to start somewhere.

I had to get this box put up and away before anybody else ended up seeing them.

"You get diaper duty. No pun intended." I pointed at Nathan and stood right next to him and whispered. "In the meantime, I've got a thousand panties with my name on them waiting to be put away."

Nathan laughed and gave me a kiss before I turned to Frank.

"A hand, please?" I asked the big bad security specialist with an attitude problem as I stood over the box.

"Yeah, close it up first though." He nearly cracked a smile.

"Alright, party people, I'm outta here. Tyler will be home soon and I wanna be there when he gets back." Rachel said before hugging me and then

Nathan's parents.

"Bye, Jords. Holler." She gave a quick wave and closed the door behind her.

Mom and Dad were headed out as well so I said my goodbyes and followed Frank down to the bedroom.

"Thanks," I said to him after he put the box on the top shelf of my ridiculously huge closet.

"No problem." He mumbled.

"Hey, what's bothering you?" I tugged on the arm of his shirt lightly.

"What isn't bothering me, Jordie? Look at everything changing overnight. Now that you kids live up here you won't need me around as much. My daughter starts college in three months and will be living in the city. She won't want me around."

"First of all, of course we'll still need you. Second, of course your daughter will want you around. And third, would it be *so* bad to go back to LA and retire? Travel with Annie. I mean, she's been one hell of a patient wife for all of these years." I nudged his arm. "You know, get in some *Frankie loves Annie* alone time. And who knows, maybe when you guys are done traveling the world you can come try out a residency on the East Coast. We aren't *all* that bad over here, after all."

"You're a good kid, Jordan. I'm sorry about earlier. It wasn't my place..."

"Stop. It's your place to say whatever you want. You kept him safe all those years before I came into the picture and then some afterwards." I linked my arm with his and led him towards the hallway.

"Not safe enough... I..." He stopped talking.

I patted his hand and left my hand over his as we walked down the hallway.

"If I don't get to blame myself, you sure as hell can't blame yourself. Nobody was prepared for what happened to him. *Nobody.*" I knew exactly what he was thinking.

He stopped and put his other hand on top of mine and made a Frank-hand sandwich.

"Are we okay now?" His eyes crinkled a bit and the stress lines on his forehead were prominent.

"We are as long as nobody finds out about that box of panties up there." I tossed my head back in the direction of the closet.

"I know a guy who can sell them on the street if you're that hard up for cash, lady." He nudged me as we walked into the hallway.

"Hell no, I bought them bitches in bulk for a reason. Keeping my name off people's asses one order at a time. That's how I got them so cheap. I bought the whole lot and promised to buy the next three." I laughed.

"Oh, Jordan." Frank shook his head and let out a quick laugh.

"I have no shame." I joked.

We stopped at the baby's room and saw Nathan had just finished changing Nate's diaper. He picked his son up off the changing table with his back to us. He began moving him up and down in front of him, making a *swoosh* sound with each movement. I got nervous and immediately walked towards him in a panic, but I stopped myself when I saw Nate smile at his daddy as he flew through the air.

*Everything is going to be all right.*

# chapter *five*

AFTER THAT FIRST DAY in the new place, the honeymoon was over. Our normal routines were back in full swing, whatever our normal was. It took a few weeks but we were finally getting settled in as a family. It was hard with Nathan gone for thirteen days but I managed. Rachel and Tyler came and stayed a night or two while he was away. Fiona took Nate on both the weekends that Nathan wasn't home, and Emma went to Kelly's, so I decided to work at the bar. I'd missed it and Rachel deserved a break. She usually only bartended on Fridays and Saturdays, but still went in nightly to close up and did payroll once a week. Besides, everyone loved a surprise visit from the boss every now and again. Right?

When I got there, the line was a typical Friday night line—halfway down the block. I had to squeeze between the railing and people to get to Mike, but I could finally see his bald head above the crowd. When he finally caught sight of me, he lifted me into a bear hug.

"Jords! I haven't seen you in forever, Jesus Christ," he yelled over the noise coming from inside when someone came through the door.

Mike put me on my feet with a huge smile on his face. "What are you doing here?"

"I had a night to myself, so I decided to come check it out. See how things are going, you know." I shrugged.

"Yeah, okay, Ms. Innocent 'Ya Know' Shoulder-Shrug. You miss being behind the bar and you miss us." He gave my shoulder a light punch.

"Yeah, yeah, whatever." I rolled my eyes and smirked. "You need to come by the new place to have dinner and see the baby. He's getting big," I shouted as I counted five people that walked out. Mike counted the next four people in line and let them in.

"I'm going to get inside. I'll see you later." I nudged him with my shoulder as I walked past him. He just laughed and I could feel his eyes on me as I went inside.

*Jesus Christ, what a zoo.*

It had been over a year since I was behind the bar on a night like this, and for whatever reason it scared the shit out of me. I suddenly felt like I couldn't breathe and I was trapped. *What the fuck, is this a panic attack?* Just as I turned to go back outside, I bumped chest to chest with Carlos, another man in my life who could pick me up like a rag doll, swing me around and squeeze me to death.

"Jordie!" He seemed genuinely excited to see me. That eased up my nerves a bit.

"Hey, buddy, long time." I smiled and hugged him back after my feet hit the floor. "Listen, think you can get me up to the bar in one piece? I'm a bit rusty," I admitted sheepishly.

"Oh, hell yeah, I can. Hop on!" He turned around and patted his back.

"What? No, you aren't giving me a piggyback ride." I laughed.

"Suit yourself. I gave you an option. Now it's my way." He grinned.

Before I could even respond, he bent and slung me over his shoulder, ass in the air, and made his way to the bar. Once we reached it, he sat me down on it. I turned around, but when I saw the hustling behind the bar, it hit me like a goddamn ton of bricks. I wasn't missed one bit back there. They were getting along just fine. In fact, the two girls behind the bar looked like Rachel and I did not too long ago. I would just be in the way if I went back there. They seemed to have everything running smoothly, people were happy, and drinks were getting poured one after another. Just as I began to turn back around, Amber caught the back of my shirt and pulled me back.

"Oh my god! How are you?" she yelled over the music and hugged me from behind. "You want some of this?" She jacked her thumb over her shoulder and smiled. "I could use an expert's hand tonight. Some of these guys are pretty ornery."

She adjusted her boobs, looked up at me, and smiled. "They look good, right? They finally dropped and settled. Feel them." She stuck her chest out.

I busted out laughing and respectfully declined.

"I'll definitely feel you up later, in the back." I winked and laughed. She laughed and stepped back so I could swing my legs over the bar and face her. Chelsea, who was one of the newer employees, smiled and reached past me.

We never did get to talk much, which felt odd because this place was my life for so long. I'd had my hands in everything when it came to this bar, and now, not only were the faces unfamiliar but so was the whole damn place. I realized at that moment, I had moved on from this part of my life and nothing would ever be the same as it was pre-Nathan. Everything had changed fundamentally and permanently…but I couldn't have been happier.

I saw Rachel round the side of the bar with some ice. She dropped it as soon as she caught a glimpse of me.

"Biiiiotch!" She slapped my leg and pulled me behind the bar. "What are you doing here, fucker? I thought you'd be watching *The Real Housewives of New Jersey* or some shit from the deluxe apartment in the sky-y-y-y," she teased.

"What the fuck ever." I rolled my eyes and laughed as I grabbed the bucket of ice and filled the bay up.

"It's nice to have you here. I've missed you…whore." She snarled playfully and teetered across the floor to some guy who looked as if he was on the verge of spontaneous combustion. He had been trying so long to get a drink that I thought he might explode.

I got back into the rhythm of things more quickly than I thought I would, and pretty soon it became the Jordie and Rachel show all over again. Regulars were coming up and chitchatting, asking how I'd been and how Nate and Emma were doing. I found it so funny that not one of the male customers asked about Nathan. *Men.* About an hour later, I noticed Amber on the floor taking orders and Chelsea cleaning tables up.

"I feel bad I showed up now," I shouted to Rachel and nodded in their direction.

"Why? If anything, you're making it easier on them. They're getting more shit done being on the floor than back here. Everything they're cleaning up now, they don't have to clean up later. You know how that goes. Plus, look at Amber—taking orders, coming back here and making them herself. Pretty fucking efficient if you ask me. I'm happy you're here." She uncapped three beers and poured a bunch of shots.

When she turned her attention back to the customer, I handed one of the regulars his beer.

"It's on me, Ben. Good to see you again." I smiled at him and got a wink in return before he walked off. I grabbed the rag and began to wipe up the mess Rachel had left from the obnoxious amount of shots she just poured. Someone started shouting something at me.

"Oh, girrrrlllll, if drinks are on you then pour me two more," she said in a southern twang I would recognize anywhere. It was Nathan's publicist and manager.

*Naomi? What the…? She should be with Nathan in LA.*

I looked up and smiled at her, because no matter how much she thought she blended in, the woman just stuck out like a gorgeous sore thumb. Naomi owned a room when she walked in. I don't know exactly what it was about her, but she turned heads everywhere she went. Even Amber had stopped dead in her booby tracks to admire Naomi. She just had it all.

"What are you doing here? I thought you were in LA with Nathan. Is everything okay?" I rattled off the questions.

"Everything is perfectly fine, beautiful. I just got done a few days early is all. Now, can a girl get a drink at this rodeo or what?" She smacked her hand on the bar with a smile.

"What can I get ya?" I had to practically scream back to ask her even though she was in my face. The crowd had jacked up about three decibels in just a few moments' time.

"How about a shot of whiskey and a Manhattan to chase it down with. A little bit of then and now."

"Sure thing." I obliged by grabbing some shot glasses and a bottle of Southern Comfort. When I turned back around I caught a glimpse of a group of people obviously checking something out. I asked Naomi to hang on a second so I could find out what it was. If there was a fight brewing, I wasn't having that shit. When I hopped on the bar to get a look, I noticed people taking pics and then I saw him. He was here, my husband, my Nathan. I was so happy I screamed his name at the top of my lungs, but he couldn't hear me.

"Why didn't you tell me he came back with you?" I said to Naomi, who by this time had poured her own shots.

"I think he wanted to surprise you, although he wasn't too happy when he came home to an empty place. He took me up to say hi to you and show me the new place. Once you didn't answer your cell, he knew where you'd be and he asked if I wanted to come with. So, here I am."

I chuckled at Naomi and looked back up to see if I could get Nathan's attention. He was standing and taking pictures with a bunch of women. One after another, everyone was taking pics.

I hopped off the bar and pushed through the crowd. When I got behind him, I stuck my head between him and the crowd and pushed through with my back turned toward the one chick whose hand was a little too close to my husband's ass for comfort.

"Babe!" Nathan grabbed me around the waist and pulled me in tight.

"Damn, did I miss you," he said before he ate my face in a jam-packed public place, and I loved every minute of it. We made our way up to the front and Nathan totally derailed my thoughts as he picked me up and sat me on the side of the bar. He pushed between my legs and pulled my head down to him by the back of my hair.

*Crowd? What crowd? I love this man.*

# chapter *six*

I WENT BACK TO say bye to Rachel before trying to pull Naomi off the stage to tell her we were leaving. When I saw she was busy dancing with some guy, I just signaled to the door and waved goodbye. She nodded and waved and motioned like she'd text me. I nodded back and Nathan led the way out. Carlos made a path for us to walk in front, but when there was a sudden hand on my shoulder from behind, I jumped and let out a startled scream.

"It's just me, kiddo." Frank chuckled.

"Jesus, Frank!" I yelled.

Carlos shook Nathan and Frank's hands and gave me a hug.

"It was good to see ya, boss lady. I know it must be hard to make the trip from the Uppa' East Siiiide to us Village folk," he teased.

"Whatever." I smacked his arm.

"Nah, I'm just playin'. I hope you know that. I'm happy for you. We're all happy for you." He pointed his chin towards the bar.

Mike gave me a hug goodbye and shook Nathan's hand, which I know was hard for him, because he wasn't Nathan's biggest fan. I don't think he knew I was aware of how he felt, but I was, and I admired him for always being so cordial. When we got to the sidewalk, I stopped and looked left. As I stared at our old place, I let out an involuntary sigh.

"Want to go check it out? Make sure everything is all right in there? No leaky pipes or anything?" Nathan asked.

"Nah, it's okay. I'm just so happy you're home early." I gave him a sheepish smile, locked my hand with his, and started towards the car waiting for us at the curb. He stood stationary and tugged me back to him. It tripped me up for a second but I caught my footing pretty quick.

"What are you doing?" I laughed when he pulled me to his chest and looked down at me.

"You know, not *all* bad happened there." He flashed me a nut-job smile and I just about melted.

"I know."

"Hold on, I have an idea." He motioned to Frank that we'd be a minute and I saw Frank roll his eyes and get back in the car. "Okay, humor me. Stand here and count to twenty. Then walk to the stoop. When you get there, you'll know what to do." He grinned.

"Nathan, no, really…," I began, but he was already walking backwards smiling—so big.

"Count," he ordered me with a quick laugh.

I must have looked pretty fucking stupid standing in the middle of the sidewalk smiling and counting out loud.

"Seventeen, eighteen, nineteen, twenty. Ready or not, here I come," I said quietly as I began walking towards our old building.

Then I saw him. He was sitting on the steps just like that first night. He was right. I knew what to do.

"Fuck," I blurted out as I got closer to him.

"Is that a statement or a request?" He grinned.

"Oh, that's a promise, Mr. Harper." I walked straight to him and straddled him on the steps.

"Wow, I'm impressed. You brushed up on those flirting skills, didn't you?" he teased.

"I love you," I said, and then mouthed the words 'nut-job.' He busted out laughing and pulled me in closer.

"I love you, too, Mrs. Harper."

Just as he landed a quick kiss on my nose, the noise level began to rise. "Shit, and so it begins," I said and climbed off him. "To be continued…"

"Um, yeah, right there in that car." He nodded at the parked car.

"Yeah, right. Cranky Franky won't have any hanky panky happening on his shift. Besides, you know he gets all bent about how others have to sit on those seats." I laughed as I pulled his hand to help him up.

I realized then that the elevated crowd noise was still over by the bar and nobody was near us. We stopped at the edge of the sidewalk and could see Mike and Carlos trying to break the crowd up. I caught a glimpse of a fight breaking out. When it started to look like it was getting out of hand, Frank hopped out to help. Luckily they got the situation under control before it escalated and Nathan and I were by our car watching the whole thing. The night I met Nathan replayed in my mind. That was the last night of my old life. I slipped under Nathan's arm and snuggled against him. Funny thing was…I didn't miss it as much as I thought I would.

When we pulled up to our building, the doorman didn't even look our way until I said hello to him. As we walked past him, I heard Frank say something about keeping his eyes forward.

"Jesus, Frank. You're going to make them hate us," I stated.

"Don't worry about it. You shouldn't care if a punk-ass kid like that hates you or not. Trust me. He's bad news. The only reason he has a job here is because his grandfather is on the committee and vouched for him. Now, I'm headed out. If you need me, you know where I'll be."

"Wait, Frank, do you want to come up for coffee?" I asked and Nathan nudged me in the back.

I didn't look back at him. I just gave him a quick nonchalant nudge back with my foot.

Frank laughed and declined. He said he was tired and going to try to get some paperwork finished. He was selling the Middletown office to one of his men who retired from the Navy.

"Thank you though, Jordan. I won't intrude on anymore of you guys' time. I'm thankful you two waited until you were out of the car, at least." He chuckled and nodded his head goodbye.

"See you two Sunday."

I guess he knew, since we had the place to ourselves the rest of the weekend, we wouldn't be going anywhere. Frank scored an A+ in the intuitive department.

One of the bad things about living in a building like ours, especially at times like this, was the elevator ride. It was damned near unbearable because of the cameras. It seemed like the longest ride *ever* while you waited with anticipation to get fucked seven ways 'til Sunday. But then again, the cameras could only catch so much.

As soon as we got in, Nathan led me against the wall under the camera hole and pressed against me. Camera or not, in a minute it wouldn't have mattered because we would have fogged up the lens. Evidently, the ride up is much quicker when you're preoccupied. We got out of the elevator and kissed our way to the apartment door. He slammed me up against it, our lips never parting, as he dug in his jeans pocket for his keys.

Once inside, we fumbled and stumbled our way around the apartment, leaving a piece of clothing at every bump. It was nothing like the choreographed love scenes you see in the movies. It was way better. It was the all-over-the-place, hanging-and-sliding-off-things, I'll-be-sore-for-the-next-five-days, is-someone-being-bludgeoned-to-death-in-there kind of lovin'.

When we finished round one an hour later with a quick shower, we headed up to give the new rooftop a try. I wasn't allowed up there until Nathan was finished with whatever project he was working on, and lord knows it took him long enough, but it was well worth the wait. Nothing could have prepared me for what I saw. Nothing. Aside from the wall and view being considerably higher—and different—it was set up to look just like my old rooftop, but with a few perks the old one didn't have. The lights, the hanging lamps, even the furniture and our lounge swing were all the same. Set up identically, he'd added a stone and glass gas fireplace with a grilling station to the left of it, all against the wall. It was the same.

I stood stunned for a moment. Then, as I walked by Rachel's and my chairs, I ran my hand across the seats. Those chairs carried a lot of memories on them, and they'd know *way* too much if they could hear.

"See, I even had your chairs set up here for you two."

"Thank you, baby. Thank you so much." I jumped up, wrapping myself around him before kissing him slowly.

He brought me to the ground. I was going to let him have his way with me again. This time though, I'd try to keep it down so not all of the Upper East Side would hear us. I let him set the pace. After all, he was the one who needed to recover from the last hour and—*Jesus Christ*— I'm so glad I did.

Before Nathan, I would seriously laugh at women who'd say they would get all out of control and have multiple orgasms just from the passion of a kiss or a touch in the right spot. I knew they were lying because I never experienced that. Shit like that only happened in movies. All that changed in a flash and I became one of those women the first night Nathan and I slept together. I was hooked. He was my undoing, and he was taking me there again.

He kissed my neck, worked his way down, and found me. My body responded before he even touched me. I arched my back, pushing against his mouth as his fingers explored me.

He looked up with those blue eyes, smiled, and I was done. I didn't give a flying fuck if all five boroughs and Hoboken could hear me. He wrecked me. I whimpered a bit as I tried to get him out of his pants and into me, but he pulled back and grinned.

"Nope. Not yet." He kissed my nose and stood up.

"Did you just deny me?" I whined when he gave me his hand and pulled me off the ground.

"I'd never deny you… I'm just delaying you for the moment." His lopsided grin gave me the warm fuzzies everywhere. He took my hand and led me across the patio.

"Toe-may-toe, toe-mah-toe, buddy." I laughed and followed his lead.

He had everything set up for us over by our big wooden lounge swing. When I went to get in it, I noticed a leather-covered journal sitting on the end table.

"What's that?" I asked as he settled in next to me.

"*That* is something I've been waiting until we moved to share with you, but you've been such a hump-a-saurus lately I haven't had the chance to show you." He grinned and picked up the journal.

"A what? A hump-a-saurus? Seriously, that's a Rachelism. You did not come up with that on your own." I laughed and reached over to smack him in the arm.

"I assure you, I did." He laughed and handed me the book.

"Hey, it takes two to be a hump-a-saurus, so I don't want to hear it. Plus, I never once heard you complain." I held the book above my face with one hand and ran my other hand over the leather cover.

"What is it?" I asked and moved to open it.

"Nuh-uh. Not yet. Once you see what it is, I don't want you to feel obligated to indulge in it. Pick it up, put it down, read it together, talk about it, or don't talk about it. Whatever *you* choose, I'm okay with it." He let go of it.

"Nathan, you're freakin' me out. What is it?" My voice cracked a bit when I asked, staring into those blue eyes that assured me I was the most loved woman in the world.

"It's my journal...from when I... It's my journal of everything that happened throughout my memory loss. From realizing I wasn't Lucas Black, right up to the last night. I didn't know why, but I had to find who was in that apartment because they were the missing piece. *You* were the missing piece, Jordan."

All I could hear was my heart pounding in my ears over my breathing as I watched his lips move.

"This is everything. I want you to know how I found you again."

For a long while, I lay there speechless.

Nathan broke the silence. "Jordan?"

He smiled as he searched my eyes.

*Do I want to go down this rabbit hole? Of course, I do...but part of me doesn't because of the other women. He said he didn't have sex with them, but still...can I handle knowing about them?*

"Jordie, say something. Please." He looked away.

I could see he was beginning to doubt the choice he made to show it to me, and I snapped out of it.

"I'm sorry. Yes, of course. I'm just having an emotion overload." I chuckled. "I never asked you about any of this...and..."

"I know you didn't. This is my way of letting it all go. It was sort of difficult to do it in the apartment, so I wanted to wait until we moved." He kissed my forehead.

I opened it. On the inside cover, there was an inscription.

*Finding Nathan.*
*Love, Mom and Dad*

# chapter *seven*

IT HAD TO HAVE been a good half hour we lay there in the lounger, listening to the sounds of the city. Nathan was rocking us back and forth with one foot hanging over the edge. My head was on his chest. I held the leather-bound journal to my chest with my hand. If it weren't for him moving his foot, I'd have thought he was asleep. It wasn't an uncomfortable silence or anything; I think it was a mutual silence. I think I was mentally preparing to take it all in and he was mentally preparing to let it all out.

"Do you think I'll be able to handle this?" I asked him.

He stopped rocking us but didn't say anything at first. Finally, he said, "Do you think you'll be able to handle this?"

"I asked you first." I gave a tight-lipped smile with a non-enthusiastic chuckle.

"Shouldn't you be asking yourself that question, Jordan?" He sounded frustrated.

"Hey, don't be like that, Nathan. I wasn't exactly prepared for this."

He sighed loudly and raked his fingers through his hair. "Babe, I wouldn't have given it to you if I didn't think you could handle it. I don't think you fully understand how I see you. You are not just this smart, sexy, gorgeous vixen that I would like to keep in bed all day, every day, might I add. You… You are the strongest person I have ever known. *Ever*. I mean, I had a pretty good idea you were one tough broad when I saw you take a hit like a champ. I'm still impressed by that shit, by the way." He gave a quick laugh and then he turned his head to look at me. We were nose to nose.

"That's right, look at these guns," I joked and kissed my flexed bicep. He took my hand, leaving my other one still across my chest, holding the journal.

"You have balls of steel but you aren't very strong. Remember, I'm the one that held you back when you went after him." He chuckled. "I mean, you're mentally strong. You had to have one hell of an ability to put mind over matter to get up after he clocked you. Jordan, he hit you like a man and you weren't going to let him get the best of you. *That* takes an incredibly strong person. At that very moment, I knew you were different. You were the one that could handle all my baggage. All the craziness, the fans, the paps. All of it. So, yeah, I think you can handle *this*."

"Jesus Christ, I asked a simple question. A yes or no would have sufficed." I laughed and handed him the journal. "Put this on the side table, please."

He took the journal, set it down, and then he crinkled his eyebrows with sadness.

I gave him my best reassuring smile. "I love you, and thank you. You'll do this with me, right? Like, if I have questions and stuff?"

"Yep. Anything you need."

"What if I get mad or jealous or whatever? Are you going to get mad at me and say I'm being ridiculous?"

"I counted on two of those three things but *whatever* is a lot of ground to cover."

"Shut up. You know what I mean." I smiled awkwardly.

"I do, and I won't. I promise."

"Good, because I need some of you right now." I leaned in and kissed him.

He kissed me back and then rolled out of the lounger.

"Where are you going?" I pouted while I tried to scoot closer to where he was standing.

He waited, gave me a hand, and then he picked up the journal.

"I'm starving. Woman, go cook me something."

He laughed at how I clumsily climbed out of the lounger. "Cheese omelet?" I asked.

"Nah, just unwrap me a Pop-Tart and call it a night." He winked.

"I think the pizza place is open until three on Friday nights. They stay open for the bar rush," I said, but quickly realized we didn't live near the pizzeria anymore.

"I'll take care of it," he said when we reached the door to go inside.

Once we were back in the apartment, he grabbed his phone and disappeared into the other room. I picked up my phone. I had a few texts. One was from Fiona—a picture of Nathan's dad in the recliner with Nate on his chest. Both of them out cold. Then there was another one from her of almost the identical picture except clearly it was a picture of an old photograph. The text that came with it said: Nearly 28 years ago. I hope you kids have a relaxing weekend. See you Sunday.

The next text was from Rachel: Tonight was fanfuckingtabulous. Please tell me we r gunna do that again soon. K? <3

I smirked as I texted her back: Do you know that Nathan said 'hump-a-saurus'?! Stop teaching him words like that. LOL. And yes, it was a blast, and yes, we'll do it again soon. <3

Rachel: Three points for the hot shot! I didn't teach him that. LOL

I woke up the next morning on my own. No alarm, no baby crying, no Emma needing to know where her hairbrush was. Nada. At first, I thought for sure I was dead. I was in a huge bedroom I hadn't fully acclimated to yet, there was a thin stream of light coming through the gigantic curtains, and just…silence.

Then the banging on the wall began and I knew all was well. One of

Nathan's button-down dress shirts was hanging over the chaise lounge by the window. *Yes, there's a fucking chaise lounge by my windows. The floor-to-ceiling windows.*

I picked up the shirt, slipped it over my head, and grabbed a pair of panties out of my drawer. When I started to make my way to what we refer to as the 'spare room,' the banging stopped and turned into a clanging of sorts.

"Whatcha' doin?" I poked my head in and saw Nathan was adjusting some sort of bracket on the wall.

"I…" He paused while he grunted, adjusting the bars. "I am putting up the TV mount." He stopped and smiled.

"Well, it sounds like you're wreckin' the joint." I walked over to him.

"Wait, we only have the three TVs. What's this for?" I looked confused.

"I'm going to make this a media room: movies, theater seats and surround sound. He was very animated and very excited.

He was beaming.

"I like the sound of all of that." I pulled him against me. "Will there be a big concessions stand in here?" I pointed behind me. "One I can hop up on and…sit…and watch you…I mean, the movie?" I said it slow and teasingly.

"Well, there will be now." He grabbed me by my behind and lifted me up so I could wrap my legs around him. "Oh, woman, you and that messy hair in my shirt, wrapped around me. Are *you* trying to kill me now?" he joked.

I let my legs drop and hopped down. "That's not funny. At all." I looked up at him.

"It was a joke, Jordan. If you and I can't make light of it, we'll never move past it."

"I thought giving me the journal was us moving past it?" I said, gathering my hair to one side and shifting to lean on my other foot.

He stood and kissed my forehead. "Go get yourself some coffee and meet me back in bed." He winked and playfully shoved me off.

"I'm not in—" I started, but he put his hand over my mouth to shush me.

"Just trust me. Get the coffee. We are going to read for a little bit before all the stuff for this room gets here."

"The stuff for this room is being delivered today? When did you begin to plan all of this?" I stopped at the doorway and turned to him.

"Why do you think I wanted at least five bedrooms *and* an office?"

"Oh yeah, heh. It never clicked. But wait, what's the office for? And there's still an extra bedroom." I must have had the most confused expression on my face because it made him bust out in a short laugh.

"I was thinking about seeing if it could be used for my assistant when I finally get to hiring one. Since it's in the front of the apartment and has a mini kitchen, a wet bar, and a bathroom, nobody will have to go traipsing through the place," he said while he picked up the tools and put them in a toolbox I had no idea we even had.

"That's fine. As long as she isn't psycho, I'm cool with it. I'll see you in bed." I gave him a shy smile. I leaned back, holding onto the doorjamb, and swung myself out into the hallway.

I was petrified. I just had to trust Nathan was right about me being strong enough. As much as I wanted to know, I didn't want to know.

I made it back to our bedroom before Nathan did. I arranged all the pillows so I'd be comfortable and ready. Then I got up and rearranged them again, got back in bed, and was up one more time for what would be a quick pee and pillow arrangement. I was like the dog circling on the blanket and digging at it until it was just right. *Finally,* I settled back in and cleaned my glasses. I could hear Nathan coming down the hallway, finishing up a phone call, I guessed. Either that or he was discussing delivery times with himself.

"Yep, sounds good, man. See you around four." He tossed his phone on the chaise and dove on top of me, destroying my perfect pillow arrangement.

"Nayy-ayayay-thannnn. I just got them right." I tried to scooch out from under him but he wasn't budging.

"Oh no, watch out, the pillow destructor is here to wreck your serious pillow business," he said in a monster voice, laughing. He let the full weight of his body come down on me, causing all the air to whoosh out of my lungs at once. I caught my breath and laughed with him.

"I'm serious, dammit! Do you know how many times I fixed those?" I wriggled under him.

"Three. Once, twice, got up to pee, then a third time, and now it'll be four—I'm assuming—after I take advantage of you."

"No advantage-taking right now. We are going to start this. Otherwise, Crasty McNasty here will keep on procrastinating." I pointed to myself.

"All right, I was just testing you anyhow. I would *never* take advantage of you." He had that shocked 'who me?' expression and then rolled over so I was on top of him and he was poking me.

"Oh, c'mon now. How do you expect me to allow a perfectly good hard-on go to waste?" I said as I rubbed up against him.

He grabbed my hips and began moving me back and forth. *Who am I to complain?*

"You sure you don't wanna work off some of that tension before we dive into this headfirst?" He actually bumped up on me when he said the word "head."

"Sending subliminal messages, are we?" I nudged him back the best I could from my position.

"Why, is it working?" He grinned and pulled me down to him by the front of my shirt.

"I am the luckiest man in the world. And I'm not just saying that because I'd like a blow job or anything…" His smile turned into a shit-eating grin as I sat up to look at his face. "I say this only because you give the *best* blow jobs."

He busted out laughing and covered his face with his forearms in defense because he knew what was coming.

"Oh my god," I shrieked as I grabbed the first pillow I could get my hands on and started to whack him with it. I'll admit my face felt like it had turned bright red.

He flipped me back over and pinned me down by my wrists.

"I mean it. I'm the luckiest man alive. I love you so much. So. Much." He loosened his grip, only to run his fingers down my arms and over my breasts, where he undid the first few buttons, exposing me. He sucked in a deep breath as he took one of my breasts in his hand and bent down to kiss me.

I had no willpower when it came to him. Nathan, the pillow destructor, was the love of my life.

# chapter *eight*

I'm not sure what I'm supposed to say here because I'm not really sure of anything. This is what I do know, though.

My name is actually Nathan Harper, not Lucas Black as I had previously believed.

My parents brought me home from a hospital in NYC about a week ago. I was shot and—from the looks of it—beaten within an inch of my life. Fortunately, I made it home in one piece—well, minus one spleen. That doesn't bother me as much as the bullet hole in my side I've got going on here.

I'm 27, soon to be 28.

I'm an actor—a popular one, apparently.

My best friend's name is Tyler.

His girlfriend is sort of nuts. No, seriously, she looks at

**43**

me like she is trying to penetrate my brain when she isn't giving me the stink-eye. I wonder what the hell I did to her in the past.

So, pretty much all I know is I have a hell of a gash on my head, I was definitely shot and nobody will tell me what the hell happened. They keep telling me that it's something I need to remember on my own. They can't put thoughts and ideas into my head. I have to figure out everything about "The Incident" without being pushed to remember.

I can only remember bits and pieces of things.

I know my parents are my parents because I can see chunks of them in my mind. With Tyler it's the same thing; there are bits and pieces that somehow fit in there. Being a celebrity is sort of hard to wrap my head around because I don't really remember much of that at all. I thought a character I played was my real life there for a few days, so yeah. It's one I'm trying to get a handle on.

My mom suggested I watch a few of my movies—that perhaps it will shake things up a bit in my mind. I beg to differ... I think things are shaken up quite enough.

Above all, I can't lose this hollowness I'm feeling inside. I'm told it's "normal" and, once it all starts coming back to me, it will fill in. For now, I need to work on it just like a puzzle. Put the edges together first then work on filling it in from there...one piece at a time.

I flipped the journal over and placed it on my lap, spine up, and drummed my fingers on it for a few seconds. I turned to Nathan who was lying on his side, head propped up on his elbow, pulling at a stem of a feather poking out of the down comforter.

"So?" he asked and looked up at me.

I could normally read his expressions easily but, for the life of me, I couldn't figure out what was going through his head.

"Well, it's a lot like what I thought you were going through at the time. I think that's to be expected, no?" I questioned.

"What do you mean by that?" He sat up against the headboard and adjusted himself.

"Well, what I mean is, all of it was to be expected. The bits and pieces, the memories, the only thing that didn't cross my mind was you feeling hollow. I can totally understand that now, but then, not so much. I guess because the last words you said to me at the hospital were, 'Now, I need my rest. If you aren't going to blow me, get out.'"

"I said that?" His eyes almost popped out of their sockets.

"You… You don't remember the hospital? Like, at all?" I was shocked.

"Nope, the first thing I remember was a day or two after getting home from the hospital and we were staying at a hotel. I woke up, went into the living area and said, 'Hi, Mom.' And she busted out in tears. I didn't know what the fuck was going on but I for sure wasn't about to start asking questions at that point. After a few sobs, she walked over and hugged me a bit too tightly. I winced and she apologized, then asked me my name. With that, I was positive she'd lost her mind so I said it slowly: 'Nathan.' She hugged me again gently and sobbed silently. She just kept saying, 'That's right. Your name is Nathan.' And from that day forward I started putting the pieces together."

"What was it like when something would come back to you? Was it like you had to work to make sense of it or did you know what it was immediately?"

"It was both. For instance, take my mom and dad. Right away, I knew who they were as soon as it came back to me. It wasn't like it was a thought in my mind, *then* I said out loud—'Ohhh hey, yeah, I remember you.' It was more like I went to bed not knowing but woke up and it just came out of my mouth. A lot of things were like that," he explained.

"Heh," I responded as I stared off at the wall.

I'd had so many questions rattling through my head for so long and now that he was answering them, I questioned again if I really wanted to know or not. Maybe he sensed that, because he took the journal off my lap and closed it up.

"Perhaps later on, or tomorrow, we can cover some more ground with this, because, honestly, the only thing I want to cover right now is you." He tugged on my shirt and that got my attention. He smacked his thighs and gave me that lopsided grin he knew I couldn't resist.

After our naked morning romp around, we decided to shower, get dressed and venture out into the world for some coffee. Luck had it there was a Starbucks right across the street from our building. We couldn't go too far anyhow because the delivery people would be there in a few hours.

I was sort of excited to see what that room would look like when finished. It would take a week or two to get everything built and assembled. In the meantime, we needed to find Nathan an assistant. I certainly couldn't do it, nor did I want to. Fuck that job. Don't shit where you eat, you know?

"Good Morning, Jordie. Nate." Ryan, the barista, greeted us as he wrote our names on the cups.

Usually he'd write a little message or note on the side along with it. After they made our usual order, he handed me mine. I turned the cup to see what he wrote. It read *Keep smiling,* with a little heart next to it, followed by *You go, Glen CoCo.* I immediately busted out at the *Mean Girls* reference and he winked at me.

I completely lost my shit though when I read Nathan's cup. "And none for Gretchen Weiners."

Nathan was somewhat amused, though not nearly as much as I was, because he grumbled something when he held the door open as we left.

"What's wrong? *That* was hilarious," I said, still smiling.

"Maybe to you, because you don't see that the kid is infatuated with you." He tried to take a sip of his steaming hot coffee. I mean, it was really steaming.

"Look, he's even trying to scald me." He took the lid off and raised his cup a little. "Imagine, I survived the insane ex-husband but Barista Boy Ryan will do me in."

We both laughed. It bothered me when he'd crack jokes about Jason but I had to start letting it go too.

"Speaking of surviving: I was thinking we should totally come up with a code word. I mean had Rach and I not done the 'Holler' thing, I doubt Frank would have caught on. So we need one," I said before taking a sip of my latte—which was the perfect temperature, might I add.

"Oh, like a safe word?" His eyes lit up like the Griswolds' house at Christmas time.

"No, you perv," I joked. "Like a code word that the entire family can use in case any of us needs help but can't ask," I explained.

"I think we've reached our quota on dangerous situations for one lifetime, but I guess you never know what else could come out of the crazy-closet you have," he teased.

"I hate you." I laughed.

"Love you too," he said with a chuckle.

"Pick a word," I said as we crossed the street. I had to pick up the pace because I didn't see a cab rounding the corner at Mach nine. When we reached the sidewalk across the street, we stopped.

"Flapjack," Nathan said.

"You're hungry?" I asked, confused.

"No, the code word for daaangerrr," he exaggerated and we began walking again.

"Ohhhh." I chuckled.

"Flapjack it is then," I agreed.

When we got back, I dropped my stuff and sat on the couch. When I took another sip of my coffee, I chuckled at my cup. "Damn, that kid cracks me up and—wait a second—he is *not* infatuated with me, FYI," I insisted.

Nathan was about to comment but the phone rang.

"Saved by the bell," I mumbled.

It was the concierge calling to let us know the delivery guys had arrived and wondering if he should send them up. "Hey, I'm going to run to the bar and catch up on my quarterlies while you do your thing. I'm pretty behind."

"You do have a pretty behind." He chuckled as drank his now non-boiling coffee.

"Cute." I smirked and grabbed my purse. I stretched up on my tippy toes to give him a kiss, but before I walked out the door he gave me a smack on the ass. I let out a yelp just as the elevator dinged and opened up. The delivery guys piled out with Frank right behind them.

"Bye, babe. Talk to you later. Okay, straight through and then to the left down the hall with that, guys. The second room on the right," Nathan instructed the men. "Watch the walls, dude," was the last thing I heard him say before turning the corner.

"What's up, Frank? Everything okay?" I dug my keys out of my purse.

"Everything's fine. The doorman called to let me know there were quite a few men with a lot of boxes wanting to deliver them up here, so he wanted to check with me first."

"What, did you want to make sure Jason wasn't delivering little men in boxes to kill us?" I snorted.

"Nope, just doing my job, Mrs. Harper," he said dryly.

I snapped my head up immediately.

"Seriously?" I stared at him blankly.

He winked at me and I shoved his shoulder. "You're such a dick sometimes!"

"Where you headed?"

"The bar," I said as I pulled my keys out.

"You want me to drive you over?"

"Nope, I'm good. Thanks." I pressed the DOWN button.

# chapter nine

WHEN I PULLED UP in front of the bar, I was tempted to go up to the old place. I didn't though, because I really had no reason to. Since we'd moved, Frank had been back there a few times to check up on things. He had some belongings still stored there so he'd reported all was well. He went back to living at a hotel a block away from us, because he wanted to be close to the new place in case he had to get to us fast.

I unlocked the door to the bar and yanked it open. It seemed so much heavier now that I wasn't there as much. I walked in, flipped on some lights, tossed my crap on the bar, and made my way to my office. It didn't even feel like *my* office any longer. Rachel had turned that shit into her own personal girl cave. Everything was new, right down to the flooring. It needed a makeover but I sure did miss my squeaky chair.

I plopped in the seat, pulled the mountain of paperwork out of the only drawer I had left in there and dropped it on the desk. About seven pages in, I heard the door unlock and some light stream in. My hand immediately reached under my desk for the gun.

*Damn, girl, those instincts really kicked in. Like a ninja.*

I felt around for it and remembered Rachel had replaced the gun with some mace and a Taser gun instead. They'd confiscated both of my real guns after the whole incident with Jason. I'm lucky that's all they did. It's not like they were registered in my name or anything. They were Jason's guns.

It was obviously somebody I knew, because they had a key, but I still kept my guard up. Once I heard the familiar clickity-clack followed by, "Hellooo, bitch, don't mace me," I relaxed.

"Hey. What are you doing here so early?" I asked her as she threw her stuff on my old chair that was now stuffed in the corner.

"I have to catch up on a few things. I've been busy with Tyler's gigs and shit. What are you doing here with clothes on? Aren't the kids gone for the weekend? I figured your hills would be alive with the sound of—"

"Ok, enough. Ha ha, you're a riot." I adjusted myself in the chair, laughing.

"For reals, I didn't expect to see you. What's up?"

"Nathan is having his home theater put in today. I came down here to play catch-up on paperwork and stuff."

"A fucking home theater?" She didn't make eye contact with me while she reached across me and shuffled through some papers.

"Can I help you with something?" It was a rhetorical question. She knew I hated that shit.

"Yeah, you can get out of my chair so I can get this done, still make it to Tyler's gig, and then be back here by nine." She didn't miss a shuffling beat, just kept on.

"Your chair?" My facial expression read *Holy shit, you have BO*, but my mind was saying *Bitch, what?*

"Yes, my chair. Your chair is over there in the corner, laid to rest. Now, please, just let me get this done and I'll be out of your way." She huffed as she grabbed a folder off the filing cabinet and turned to me.

"Fine with me. I have someone coming in about an hour. New distributor. May I conduct business in my office then, boss?" I pushed away from the desk, allowing myself to roll back freely with my arms and legs extended straight out in front of me before I stood and moved out of her way.

"Holy shit, don't fucking start, Jordan. I don't give a shit what you do after I'm finished." She plopped in the chair, exhaled loudly, and put her head down.

"Rach, are you okay?" I moved my head so I could see her face but she'd buried it in her hands by then.

"I'm fine, Jords. I'm sorry. I'm just stressed."

"What can I do to help? Is it too much here? I can hire a full-time office person, Rachel. I didn't mean to keep this on you for so long. I thought I'd be back by—"

"No, it's not too much," she snapped. "I just… I'm fine."

I could have been hallucinating, but I think I saw tears in her eyes.

"Oh, for the love of all that is holy, Rachel, look at me, dammit!" I yelled.

"What? Fine, I think Tyler is cheating on me! Happy? Now *please,* let me get this shit done." She quickly clammed up again.

"I'm sure he isn't…," I began, but then thought better of it.

I knew she'd talk when she was ready, but I intended to grill Nathan when I got home.

"And keep your big fat mouth shut. *Do not* say anything to Nathan." She didn't look up at me.

"Got it." *Don't say anything, my ass.* "Rach, I love you. I'm—"

"Don't apologize for something you had nothing to do with. Love you too."

I walked out and closed the door to give her some space. She didn't need a lecture or a bitch-venting session, she needed to sort out and compartmentalize everything, digest it, and *then* she'd be ready.

When I got back to the apartment, there was still a shit ton of people there. I heard a lot of power tools and men talking over them. I poked my head in the room to look for Nathan. I didn't see him in there, but when I turned around he was standing behind me. I jumped and let out a squeal, which made Nathan laugh.

"What the hell, Nathan? You scared me. You're lucky I didn't go all kung-pow on your ass," I said, and it just made him laugh harder.

"Yeah, kung-pow alright. Kung Pao chicken is about all you'll go." He grinned and gave me a kiss. "So, get some work done?"

"I did. Actually, it felt good to take a half a load off," I answered as I walked towards our bedroom.

Nathan put down the drill he was holding and followed me.

"That's good, but I still don't get why you can't hire someone to do all that. It's an accountant's job, pretty much," he replied just as a loud thud, crash, and a few "shits" were heard coming from the media room.

"To be continued…" He rolled his eyes and kissed my nose.

"Because it's still my bar and I need to be responsible for it," I said.

"I know you do. That's my wife. The epitome of responsibility." He shook his head with a smirk.

Suddenly, we're being interrupted by one of the installation men standing at our bedroom door. "Sorry to disturb you. We have an issue," he informed Nathan.

"I heard," he responded and then looked at me. "I'll be back."

"Hey, before you go, speaking of responsibility, have you erased that stuff yet?" I shouted on my tippy toes as he headed out of the room.

"No way. Not before the media room is finished. It's all in the clouds, baby. No need to worry." He wiggled his eyebrows and followed the guy down the hallway.

# chapter *ten*

July 8th

Today would be one of those days that I'd say "I've lost my mind," but unfortunately for me... that's what happened.

It started out with waking from a dream that I couldn't remember—imagine that—but at the same time I couldn't forget it. There was something in the dream that had my brain cranking into overdrive.

I finally got my stitches taken out. Dad wanted to pull them out himself and rub some dirt on it, as the old saying goes, but Mom called him an idiot and had Frank take us to the doctor. My parents are quite the comical duo, I know that much. I hope I can have that someday.

Frank is a pretty interesting guy. He definitely knows more about me than I do. I wondered if he could give me some info, but when I asked him, he hesitated. It was like he wanted to tell me, but instead he just shook his head and said, "Some day, kid. Some day." While waiting in the doctor's office, a woman approached me for an autograph. She handed me a piece of paper with her number and Coffee one day? written on it. Mom was practically stabbing this chick in the face with her dagger-eyes and, after she walked away, went on about how trashy it was to throw herself at a man like that, especially in front of his mother. Then my mom insisted I give my brain some time to try and process and digest everything that's happened so far.

I just wanted out of this fucking hotel room and to have a conversation with someone other than Mom, Dad, Tyler or Frank. So, I called her.

We met up in the downstairs restaurant of the hotel. I thought I might actually be able to hear what the girl was saying instead of being disrupted every five minutes or hearing the paparazzi click away. Of course, Frank stood guard at the entrance. I saw him stop her as she got to the front. They spoke for a minute. Her name is Charlie, short for Charlene. She's 24 years old and works at Hooters. I like Hooters' hot wings.... and that's about all we had in common. She did eventually ask how I was feeling. I tried to play it off like I knew what had happened so I didn't seem like I was a complete vegetable. She stopped talking after that. I walked her out, thanked her for the company and kissed her on the cheek. Instantly, I felt like someone had ripped my insides out and gutted me.

I haven't been able to shake that feeling yet. I know my brain has more holes than the Moonlight Bunny Ranch but this one... This one is important. I need to find out what it's all about before I go mad.

I closed Nathan's journal and put it on my nightstand. I laid my head on Nathan's chest and just listened to him breathe for a few minutes before I ran my finger up and down his stomach.

"Any questions?" he asked as he took in a sharp breath, probably due to the close proximity of my fingers to the waistband of his boxers.

"Yes," I said flatly, slipping my hand into his boxers.

I wasn't exactly sure why I did it, because it was really out of character for me. We both knew it. We were the spur-of-the-moment couple. Something funny, playful, or passionate always led us to our sexy time, but I wasn't really sure what I was feeling. The only thing I knew at that moment was I needed to feel how much he loved me. I mean, I could *see* how much, but I suddenly felt an insecurity I've never had before. I think it was the realization that at one point Nathan really had no idea we existed. I seriously began to question if I'd be able to handle the whole journal thing. Nothing had even happened yet and my insides were already twisting.

I sat up on my knees and positioned myself between his legs. I could tell he was confused as I pulled his boxers down in the front and bent so my mouth hovered over him.

"Jordan, what are you—" he began, but before he could finish his sentence, I silently answered his question. He let out a strained hiss of pleasure and grabbed on to my hair. It was what he always did when I went down on him, but this time he guided my head up.

"Jordie, what's going on?" His blue eyes searched mine as he held my head up and rubbed it at the same time.

"Is this a problem?" I forced a grin.

"In theory, hell no…but when it comes to you and me, yes, it's a problem. Come up here." He pulled me up.

I yanked on my shirt to take it off but he stopped me. That didn't help with my issue. I wanted to scream in the worst way. I pushed his hand away and took my shirt off anyway.

"Let's talk about what's going on in there." He tapped my forehead lightly.

"You said if I didn't want to talk, it was okay. You said however I wanted to work through it, you would work through it with me." I stared down at his chest while I spoke.

"I did… You're right. Just do me one small favor, please?" He bumped his hips underneath me and I smiled because I knew he still wanted me.

"I'll try." I gave him a sarcastic grin.

"Can you tell me why this is how you want to work through it?" He ran his hands up and down my thighs as I sat there, still straddling him.

*Why? Why do I want to handle it like this? I'm Captain Crazy Pants, that's why… Somewhere in my brain I fried a circuit because I know you love me… again… now… but there was a time you didn't, and I don't know if I can deal with that.*

"I just wanna be close to you," I whispered close to his ear.

"That's good enough for me." He gripped my hips hard and pulled me as close as possible against him. Somehow, in one quick motion, he was on his knees and on top of me.

My heart was pounding. For a split second, I felt like I was being judged on a high-dive or some shit. Like my performance mattered. *What the hell is wrong with me? This is the one person who knows me as well as I know myself. He loves me… crazy pants and all.*

The moment I locked eyes with Nathan, I snapped out of it. He found the spot on my neck that drove me nuts and my hands found his hair. Now I was a definite foreplay kind of girl, but tonight I really needed it to be quick and dirty, so I did all the little things that I knew drove him nuts.

"Baby, I won't last five minutes if you keep this up," he said into my mouth as he kissed me.

"Why not?" I asked him. I needed to hear it, feel it. I needed to reassure myself, however fucking asinine it was. I needed it.

"Oh my god, woman, seriously. Holy fuck, you're gorgeous and you're all mine." He sat up on his knees between my legs and positioned himself just right before he slipped inside me. He didn't move though, he just stared down at me with the most intense look on his face. I instantly felt my face heat up and butterflies in my stomach. I tried desperately to read him as I stared back inquisitively. His lips quirked up a bit in the corner.

"I love you," he said as he brought his lips to mine.

His expression said it all—not his words, his expression.

I closed my eyes, and, in an instant, I could feel how much he loved me.

That was my undoing. I hadn't even fully finished before I felt his full weight on me. His arms wrapped under my back so his hands gripped my shoulders. He pulled me down to meet each of his thrusts. We were as close as possible and he'd gotten so deep that the aftershock came on fast and hard. I don't think I've ever had an orgasm like that before… I swear I saw colors. No shit. Colors. I may have even heard fireworks and the Star Spangled Banner.

I got up before Nathan did. It was Sunday morning, so I'd let him sleep in and made him some breakfast. Just as I was putting the bacon on a plate he walked in the kitchen.

"Morning. Hungry?" I held up a plate of bacon and eggs with some toast and handed it to him.

"Oh, hell yes. Thank you." He gave me a dopey grin and a quick kiss.

"Was I too noisy?" I asked while I got him some coffee.

"Nah, you didn't wake me up. My mom called. They'll be here about six. They're heading over to Jersey to pick up Emma and then go shopping," he said with his mouth full as he sat down at the table.

"Okay," I answered and went right into what was on my mind. "So, I had to email Rachel because she hasn't answered any of my texts—and speaking of Rachel, she was a fucking nightmare at the bar yesterday when I saw her. Has Tyler said anything to you about them having problems? Because she's convinced he is stepping out on her." I took a sip of my coffee and waited for him to finish chewing.

"What? Tyler, cheat? That is so ridiculous its borderline amusing," he said, then ate the last of his bacon.

"Well, she was bitching at me about it, Nathan. She's devastated. Can you talk to him, please? Maybe poke around a bit and see if you can find anything out?"

"Are ya done?" he asked as he stood up. "With your plate, that is." He grinned.

"Yes, smartass, I am. What do you know?" I stood up and followed him to the sink after he took my plate.

"I know nothing, Jordan. Naaahhh-thiiiing, I say." He put the plates in the sink and turned to me.

"Bullshit, you shitty liar that lies. You're lying! Tell me or I will just assume the worst and go over there and rip his arms off and beat him with them."

"It's nothing bad, I promise. He isn't cheating on her." He put his arms around my waist and kissed me.

"But she said he has been doing like triple the amount of gigs that he normally does and is never home. That's why she drives herself nuts to make it to all of his shows, because he is always working now," I informed him.

"The two of you conjure up the most elaborate shit ever. You should be writing dramedies, I swear." He poked my side with his pointer finger, pushed off the counter and walked past me to get more coffee.

"Don't change the subject, bucko. What is going on?" I demanded an answer this time.

"Jesus Christ, chill, woman. You can't say anything. It's a surprise. You promise?" He turned to me and took a sip of his freshly-poured cup of joe.

"Holy crap, Nathan, I *promise*. Now tell me," I urged and whined.

"He's going to ask her to marry him. The extra gigs have been to pay for the ring. I offered to help him out but nope… He said he had to earn it. He wanted her to see how much he loves her by how hard he worked to get to where he wants to be with her: married."

I stood there in shock. Rachel…married? That was something I never thought I'd see. Wow. Rachel married.

"Thank god. Well I hope he doesn't wait too much longer to ask, because it's killing her inside. She's really hurt."

"He planned on doing it next weekend. His mom, brother, and sister are flying in for it," he said.

"Well, damn. I hope she says yes." I laughed.

# chapter *eleven*

I WAS LYING ON my stomach next to Nathan, eye-level with his journal. I knew he saw me staring at it. I could feel his eyes on my back.

"Do you want to read a little more before we get up?" he asked me.

"No, I don't feel like moving right now."

"Well, we have to." Nathan smacked me on the ass before he got out of bed.

I stayed in bed and watched him as he put on his boxers. Jesus Christ, he was a fine specimen. He tossed me my shirt and asked if I was sure.

"Yes, I'm sure I've had enough for one day. Besides, your parents and kids will be back soon. We don't need a repeat of what happened last time." I laughed as I sat up and tossed my shirt onto the chaise.

He leaned down and kissed me.

"It'll be fine, don't worry about it. I told you we'd do this together," he said.

"That's just it, I don't know if I can read this with you. I mean, nothing has even happened yet and look how I freaked. All I could think about was sex, sex, sex, like that was the only way to hold on to you right then. How ridiculous is that?" I asked as I approached him. "And what's with the boxers?

We need a shower." I raised an eyebrow at him.

He gave me my smile and dropped his shorts.

"I won't argue with that." He grabbed me around the waist and pulled me in tight.

The kids were home and in bed by the time I was finished cooking dinner for Nathan and me.

"Dinner's ready," I called out, putting the plates on the counter.

"What's with that smile?" I laughed as Nathan approached me.

"Just happy." He shrugged as he put a piece of chicken on his plate.

"It's chicken... Nothing to get all emotional over," I teased.

He kissed my head as he grabbed his fork.

By the time we were finished eating, both kids were out cold. Nate had been sleeping through the night for about two weeks, so I knew I'd be in for an early morning. I decided to call it a night and headed to the bedroom to get changed.

I heard Nathan enter the room as I began brushing my teeth.

"I feel like we just got out of bed," I joked.

"I make a lasting impression." He walked into the bathroom and picked up his toothbrush.

"Indeed," I said after I spit.

"Sexy." He chuckled while he tooth-pasted up his toothbrush.

"I too make a lasting impression." I gave him a big cheesy smile, turned, and wiggled my butt as I walked out.

I went to go check on Nate one last time and kiss him goodnight since I didn't get to before Nathan put him down.

I knew what would be waiting for me when I got to our bedroom.

*The Journal.*

I picked it up and sat cross-legged with it in my hands.

"What? No pillow brigade tonight?" He laughed as he sat up.

"Shut it," I said as I took a pillow from behind me and put it on my lap.

**60**

"Oh, well, excuse me. I stand corrected." He chuckled and kissed the exposed skin on my shoulder as I opened the book.

July 29th

I've been getting out more and more, and remembering tidbits and chunks of myself with each passing day. I've been very careful with the company I keep. Charlie decided to tell the tabloids I was a man-whore trying to take advantage of my 'situation.' My guess is she wasn't very happy I didn't call her again. Last week, a former costar, Lena, called. We met up for coffee. That was a confusing and awkward situation, to say the least. She practically sat on my lap, touched me a lot, and held my hand when we were walking. At first, I thought it was a friendly thing, but I don't think she did. That scenario was a nightmare for me to get a handle on. Especially with the photogs everywhere. Even if they're keeping their distance. Don't get me wrong, the attention was nice and she is... Holy Christ, she's smokin' hot...but something is off. Usually when a woman like that kisses you, you have some sort of response. Mentally, physically... something. I had nothing. It was like kissing a doorknob. That kiss made the front page of US Weekly, which sent Mom into a complete shit fit. Not in front of me, of course...but I heard her talking to someone on the phone about allowing her to talk to me about something. I also heard her scolding the person on the other line for being so stubborn and selfish, but by the end of the call she'd told the person she loved 'em... which meant whoever it was on the other end of that call was important. When I asked her about it, she told me she was talking to Rachel about Tyler.

Lies. Something is up and I can FEEL it. Not just see it. Feel it.

I was silent after I closed up the journal and stared at the ceiling while I gave myself a pep talk.

*Well, fuck. That sucked. That sucked big fat Kardashian ass is what that did. UGH. Stop shaking... Get your shit together, Jordie.*

I exhaled a long, loud breath and turned to Nathan with a weak smile.

"Jordan, if this is too much... I didn't think—" he said, but I stopped him.

"I'm fine. Surprisingly enough I'm a lot better than I anticipated. Okay, yeah, that sucked. I didn't expect the whole handholding and the 'smokin' hot' part, but it is what it is. I just keep reminding myself that you didn't know I existed."

I was looking down, fixated on my hands. I was fiddling with my rings.

"I didn't...and I can't begin to imagine how you felt having to see all of that without knowing the facts." He scooted up and sat in front of me, mirroring the way I was sitting.

"Is it safe to assume it was you my mom was talking to that night?" he asked as he lifted my chin up to look at him.

"Yes," I whispered.

"How come you didn't want her to tell me about you—about us and Emma and the baby?" he asked.

And there we had it: the big Voldemort of questions... The one we had not spoken of... We'd just set sail into unchartered waters, because this was taboo as far as I was concerned. It was the past...but again, I was trying to save Nathan from the pain of knowing what brought me to the decision to keep it all a secret.

"It's your turn, Jordan. It's your turn to let it all out. I'm okay, we're okay, our family is okay. You don't have to protect me anymore," he assured me.

"I hate when you do that shit." I gave him a small smile.

"Do what?" He cocked his head to the side in question.

"When you read my mind like that."

"So?" He took my hands in his.

"There were a few reasons. At first, it was because I didn't want to cause you more confusion. You didn't know who you were, and I was going to throw at you an almost-wife, a step-kid, and a baby on the way? It's not my style. I wasn't doing that to you. Then, as you began to remember more and more but not me—or us—and I saw you continually going on dates and being affectionate with other women, I decided it was what was best for everyone. I'd move on with my life and you'd regain yours."

I sniffled because I was starting to tear up like a big fat sissy.

"You were going to keep my child a secret from me because I was dating?"

I could tell by his expression he didn't know how to react to that. He looked torn between pissed and confused.

"Don't look at me like that, Nathan. You don't understand—" I started to say, but he cut me off.

"You're damn right I don't understand." His eyebrows mashed together.

*All right, he was pissed, not confused.*

We were both silent for a moment or two.

"Help me understand. I know it wasn't out of spite or anything like that. At least I *hope* it wasn't." He rubbed the top of my hand with his thumb.

I could tell he was doing his best to keep it together and stay calm.

"When you were in the hospital—after it first happened—you said some pretty shitty things to me. They hurt and they stuck with me. So, after that, I went to *great* lengths to keep it a secret. I mean, Frank and Todd had to pay off the paps so they didn't bother us, and the police report was buried with Hoffa, I assume, because nobody ever got a hold of it. Jason wasn't having a public trial since the military was dealing with him, so…it was just easier to leave well enough alone. You wouldn't have to relive the incident and pretend you knew who I was, let alone love me and have a baby on the way." I saw his face ease up a bit.

"What did I say?" he asked.

*Fuck, fuck, triple fuck. I didn't want to do this.*

"Well, you pretty much said that you didn't know me… That you couldn't have kids because you were sterile, so the baby wasn't yours, and you already know what you said about me either blowing you or leaving. That's all I remember, because I blacked out after that. Oh, and that I was hot, and from the looks of my face I liked it rough." I began to sob after I said the last part.

I thought about how I reacted last night and how all I wanted to do was jump on Nathan to show him how much I loved him. How I couldn't have him close enough to me. Tonight, I just wanted to cry.

The thought of Lena's lips on his made my skin crawl and my stomach curl inward. I hadn't cried sad tears in a long time. It had been all happy fucking trails since he came back to me...and now...just like he'd said...it was my turn. He'd put it out there for me to understand where his head was during that time. It was my turn to let him know where my heart was during that same time.

He moved to sit next to me. He pulled me onto his lap and just let me cry. He didn't say anything; he simply rubbed my arm, moved the hair out of my face, and kissed me lightly until I cried myself to sleep. Two nights, two different reactions... We were in for one hell of a rollercoaster ride.

Nate woke up around a quarter after five and Emma shortly after. When I walked in from getting her off to school, Nathan was on the phone.

"No, Mom. I don't like to go to the Starbucks across the street. You see, the young man who has a massive crush on my wife is trying to kill me." He said obnoxiously loudly as he passed by the kitchen.

"That is not true or funny, Nathan," I yelled out to him. I heard him laugh. *Oh, how I love that man.*

# chapter
## *twelve*

FRIDAY CAME QUICKLY. SURPRISINGLY enough, I accomplished a lot. I'll be the first to admit that since we moved, life had been so much less chaotic. I didn't want to say it out loud but it was...normal. I mean, right down to being able to walk outside our building and not have a mob scene of paparazzi and fans. The fans weren't a problem most of the time anyway, but the photographers were relentless.

After a bath for Nate and a shower for me, we emerged fresh and ready for the day at nine twenty. Fiona was on her way to pick up Nate and I was so thankful because I had errands to run. I always felt bad toting him around while I ran here and there. I would rather he be with his grandparents getting some brain stimulation and activity than in a car-seat carrier all damn day.

When they arrived to pick him up, I had just gotten Nate all bundled up and ready to go. The cab was waiting downstairs for them. As we were saying our goodbyes, Rachel came barging through the front door in tears.

"Oh, Christ," I mumbled.

I wasn't prepared to deal with this. Nathan had *just* told me about Tyler's plan to pop the question, so I hadn't come up with a reassuring excuse yet.

"Rachel, sweetheart, what's wrong?" Fiona asked, concerned.

"It's Tyler. He's cheating on me," she stammered through her words and wailed out.

We were all sort of dumbfounded because it was a solar flare in the east wind on the third Tuesday of every century when you saw Rachel cry, let alone go full-blown emotional basket-case.

"Oh, Rachel. That is just ridiculous." Fiona waved her hand. "That boy is nuts about you. You're everything to him. I was just talking to his mother the other night. She called to ask about a rest..."

"She called to find out about a good remedy to get some rest, right? Me too. She called here asking how I was getting a full night's rest with the baby being up. I told her I was lucky to have a brilliant, caring mother-in-law who helps me out." I gave her the wide-eyed 'stop talking' look.

"Yes, lucky you," Fiona said.

Thank god, she got the message.

"Anyhow, Rachel, I'm sure you're just being overly sensitive. Are you due for your period?" Fiona asked, and I busted out laughing at Rachel's facial expression.

"What? No. What kind of question is that, Fiona?" Rachel said before she blew her nose.

"A legitimate one. Women tend to get a bit more emotional before their cycles." She shrugged at me like she had no idea what to do.

"Ok, time to stop talking," I snorted and gave Fiona the go-ahead to leave with a kiss to Nate and a gentle arm behind the back to guide her along.

"Bye, kids." Fiona gave Rachel a sheepish smile and left.

"What the fuck? My period? I love her and all, Jords, but for reals... She can be a wacky broad at times."

"Okay, so what's up?" I ignored what she said about Fiona and dragged her over to the couch to sit with me.

"Okay, so I was opening the mail and I accidentally opened Tyler's AMEX bill instead of mine. When I realized it was his and went to put it down, I noticed some hotel charges for the Ritz fucking Carlton, Jordan... The fucking Ritz," she yelled and threw her bag on the ground.

I went to pick it up because it was a beautiful MK bag, but she slapped my hand and told me not to. I looked up at her, startled; her face was bright red and full of snot and tears. She reminded me of myself on the night Nathan left my apartment the first time. Only she could walk and, well, function.

"Rachel, I'm sure it's for a gig or something. Maybe a label is coming in from LA to see him play and he got a room in an attempt to impress them?" I blurted out.

*Damn, girl, not too shabby for a spur-of-the-moment excuse.*

"The charges are for a reservation. When I called today, the woman told me it was booked for next weekend. The penthouse suite." She sobbed.

"He told me he had a gig late Friday night, so he wouldn't be at the bar to take me home." She cried harder and dragged out her sentence in a loud whine.

"Did you ask Nathan about it?" She shot at me and leaned in close.

"What? No. You told me not to," I said.

"Why the fuck not? You never listen to me, why did you decide to start now?"

"Okay, Rach, calm down. You're a little hysterical…," I started, but she went off on a tangent about why she "hates love" and how "men suck—they always leave."

Her dad had left her and her mom, and her only other real relationship ran off with some SoHo tramp back in 2004, so it had left her a bit jaded…and now there was Tyler with his secrets. I've never experienced being dumped… unless your fiancé not having any recollection of you or your unborn child counts. I can imagine the experience would leave her feeling cynical.

"What the hell is that noise? Rachel? Was that you? What the fuck is wrong with you and what is that noise you're making?" Nathan walked into the room and looked confused.

"She opened Tyler's credit card statement by accident and saw charges for the penthouse suite at the Ritz Carlton for next weekend." I gave him the *eek* face.

"Oh, that? I arranged for a music director to fly in and discuss the possibility of getting some of his tracks onto a soundtrack or two. I told him to pay for the room and I'd reimburse him." Nathan was calm and collected, not a single hitch in his voice.

*Damn, he's good, and on the same page as me.*

"Then why didn't he tell me?" she asked, beginning to calm down.

"If I know Tyler—and I have since I was fifteen—he didn't want to get his hopes up or jinx it or have you show up and make him nervous. He'd rather hide it than ask you not to come to show him support and risk hurting your feelings. You know?" He shrugged as Rachel sat up straight and stopped crying completely.

"Yeah, I guess." She sniffled.

*Holy shit. He pulled it off.*

"Stop that crying and go wash your face." Nathan gave her a head nod towards the bathroom. "While she does that I have to go back and assure Frank that a cat was not on fire out here."

He turned to head back down the hallway.

"Hey," I said to get his attention back over to me.

"Thank you," I mouthed when he turned around.

"You're welcome," he mouthed back and winked.

# chapter *thirteen*

Making new/old friends is great. Tyler and Rachel took me out to eat one night, and the waitress was cute, so I saw no harm in asking her out for drinks or whatever came to mind afterwards. Before she could even answer, Rachel made a remark about me waiting until my rash clears up before I get back out there. I have no fucking clue what that was all about...but it sure pissed me off.

Mom and Dad have to go back to Sacramento for a week or so pretty soon. She wants me to come with them. I don't want to hurt her feelings, but I need a break from her. Dad's motto is, "It is what it is and what will be, will be." Mom doesn't seem to get that. Things are also getting tense between us, so it'll be good for her to be away from me for a while. For now, I've stopped asking what happened. If I haven't remembered by now, there's a reason I don't remember. The puzzle is slowly getting put together day by day. More and more comes back to me... Sometimes it's a smell, sometimes it's nothing in particular— just a random memory. I've come to terms with the fact that there is a reason my brain doesn't want to me to know. Whenever I ask anyone I'm dating, they just tell me that nobody really knows what happened—just that I was shot and lost my memory. Besides—the women I hang out with—most of them are really great ladies, but by the third date I realize that something isn't there and the void inside remains empty.

August 14th

Today Tyler took me over to the studio. I've been in talks to start working again soon. I've been looking at projects and whatnot, but I'm still not cleared to drive. They suspended my license for six months. The doctors said it's a mandatory precaution because I had a seizure in the hospital. I think it's a mandatory pain in my ass. Mom and Dad are leaving for Sacramento tomorrow. I have a date tomorrow night. I met her at the gym over at the studio. She works in the legal department. She seems nice enough, so I asked.

Tyler says I need to slow down. I guess to him it looks like I actually am being a man-whore, fucking every hot chick I see. I'm just hoping to get some quality alone time with a woman. It's been so difficult knowing there are people watching me at all times. If it isn't the paps, it's Frank; if it isn't Frank, it's Mom; if it isn't Mom, it's Tyler. And it's CONSTANT.

Let's see how this one goes.

# H. J. Harley

It's 9:10 p.m. and I'm home from my date. Yes, already!

I wanted to get out of the city to a place a little less expected, so Frank said he had the perfect spot. It was a pizza joint over in the East Village. That part of town was like its own little world. So many people but not too crowded. When I got out of the car to help Sadie (the chick I met in the gym), something caught my eye. Well, it didn't exactly catch my eye—it was actually more like a flash of something. I was frozen...completely blank. Then, suddenly, it was like somebody shook my head and scrambled everything around again. I couldn't focus and I felt like running because the void in my gut was swallowing me whole. I kissed Sadie on the cheek, apologized to her, and asked Frank to take her home.

Something about that place was a game-changer for me. I walked around for what felt like hours but still couldn't figure out what I was missing. I stopped in a bike shop and bought one to ride. Something important is there. I just have to figure out what.

August 16th

Frank came to pick me up this morning. I stopped at Tyler's. His girlfriend went postal about me showing up unannounced. She yelled, "What if I'd had company or hadn't cleaned?" I reassured her that I didn't mind if it wasn't clean, and I told her I don't bite people, but she just stood there. It was pretty evident Rachel was not happy about it, but I'm glad she wasn't; otherwise she wouldn't have thrown a boot at Tyler, and I wouldn't have remembered a boot just like it...blood stains and all.

When I picked it up, Rachel just stared at me...HARD.

Like she was trying to send me some kind of telepathic message...or shrink my head. It was very strange. Tyler took the boot and laughed. When I asked about a boot with a blood stain, Rachel's whole demeanor changed. She smiled at me and began to talk, but Tyler quickly interrupted. Rachel rolled her eyes and left the room.

Rachel knows more than what everyone's letting on. I know she'll crack. She's one to spontaneously combust if you shake her up enough.

Later, I went for a bike ride and ended up back at the pizzeria. I was hungry, so I went in for a slice. The waiter asked how I was doing like he knew me. He asked where my bodyguard was. Why he would give a shit about that is beyond me. But he did tell me that Frank could be a scary guy.

I rode my bike around, up and down the streets. Three hours later, I was sitting on a street bench on East 13th street. I didn't know why.

I put Nathan's journal back in its normal place on my nightstand after I closed it. I wanted to slam it shut but I refrained.

"Is it getting any easier for you?" Nathan took my hand and raised it to his lips.

"I feel like I should be saying yes...," I responded in a hushed voice.

"I feel like you should be saying exactly how you feel." He kissed my hand and put it on his stomach.

"Okay then. Yes and no. Yes, because I am getting used to the fact that there were other women...and no, because I get the same desperate pit in my stomach every time I read something about one of them. Make sense?" I peered over at him.

"Perfect sense." He exhaled and stared up at the ceiling. "Would you like to continue?"

"Stop asking me the same shit every time I'm done. I'll let you know when I've had enough," I snapped, then swung myself so I was sitting on the edge of the bed.

"I'll take that as a no," he mumbled.

"Why?" I stood and headed to the bathroom.

"Because you're walking away." He gestured with his hand.

"I have to pee, Nathan. Jesus Christ." I spun around to look at him.

He raked both his hands through his hair and grabbed two fistfuls while a long, seemingly frustrated rumble erupted from the back of his throat.

"My god, you frustrate the hell out of me, Jordan." He jerked his hands from his hair, slapped them on his lap, and exhaled loudly.

"I can see how my need to urinate can be distressing and frustrating to you."

I rolled my eyes and slammed the bathroom door behind me. I hurried up and peed because I knew he'd be walking through the door at any moment. Just as I expected, he came in right after I flushed.

"Sorry," he said as he leaned on the wall next to the open door.

"You have nothing to apologize for, Nathan."

I reached into the shower to hit the button that turned it on. It was one of those fancy mammojammos, where you wave your hand by the sensor and adjust the temperature digitally. Or, in my case, hit button number one, the one already programmed to my preferred water temperature. Talk about ostentatious.

Nathan stuck his hand in and hit button number three, which meant a shower for two coming up. That was our agreed upon temperature. I wrapped my hair up in a signature Jordie half-assed bun and waited for the beep. Just like an oven, it fucking beeped when it preheated to the proper temperature. I eyed Nathan carefully as he undressed. I had to choose my words wisely because I didn't want him to take the journal away from me, but at the same time I didn't like the direction it was heading in.

I stepped in a few seconds shy of the beep and Nathan followed.

"You know what I was just thinking?" I said to him as I grabbed the soap.

"What's that?" he answered while he wet his hair.

"I'm afraid if you don't like what I have to say about something in your journal, you're going to take it away from me." I lathered up my arms.

"That's ridiculous. You don't think I took that into consideration beforehand, Jordie? Of course I weighed the ramifications of sharing it with you, but I told you already I know you can handle it." He began to shampoo his hair so he wasn't looking at me.

"That's great but not what I'm saying. I know I can handle it…but can you deal with the way I handle things?"

He opened his eyes, stared at the ceiling, and stopped washing his hair for a moment before chuckling.

"If you and I could get through that, we can get through anything. So, yeah, I'll be okay." He started to rinse.

"Just as long as we're on the same page… No pun intended." I hip-checked him, and he grabbed me around my waist and pulled me close.

"I hope we're on the same page." He leaned in and kissed me.

"Hold on, tiger…" I looked down because I could feel him against me. I tippy-toed up to kiss him.

"You know, Rachel told me about the day you stopped by unannounced. She really thought you would remember at any moment once you saw my boots. She wanted it to happen so badly. Everyone was tired of seeing me a total mess." I turned away from him so he could wash my back.

"Well, it's not like you made it easy for me to remember, Jordan." He snickered playfully. "You wouldn't let anyone talk about you. Frank had to pay off every media outlet to *not* mention you at all, and then threw a medical gag order at the ones who didn't want to comply. The mental damage I could endure by being force-fed any information about us or the pregnancy… It was as if everyone thought it could set off some emotional chain reaction and Nathan goes boom," he rattled off in one quick sentence as his hands rounded to the front of me, sliding over my breasts.

I leaned my head back on his chest and closed my eyes.

"I had my reasons, Nathan. Mainly because I didn't want you to 'go boom,'" I said to him.

"What if I'd never remembered? Were you going to just never tell me about Nate?" He slid his hands down to my waist and kept them there.

I opened my eyes and stared off in silence. *Uh-oh…*

"Tick-tock, tick-tock." He nudged into me from behind.

"I didn't think that far ahead. It was a bridge I planned to cross when we got there, ya know?" I said in a shaky voice.

"You okay?" He turned me around.

"Yeah—" I paused "—I'm hungry."

I lied.

"I love you, Jordan. No matter what." His eyes locked with mine.

Lord, what those blue eyes still did to my insides.

"I love you too," I replied.

I was sex-spent and pleasantly sore by the time Sunday morning rolled around. Nathan and I had one hell of a weekend together.

Emma was going to be home around noon and Fiona was on her way back with the baby. Nathan made waffles, so, when I got out of the shower, it was all I could smell in the air. This girl loved her husband's waffles.

"Smells *so* good," I said to Nathan when I walked in the kitchen.

I hopped up on the counter next to where he was waffle-making and my shirt hitched up so that he could see my panties.

"As much as I'd like to have you for breakfast, I regretfully have to resist and ask you to put some pants on." He bent and kissed the top of my thigh and looked back up with a smile.

*Look at his eyes. Yum. What I*—"Jordan." He snapped his finger and chuckled.

"Yeah? What? Huh?" I sat up straight, wide-eyed, and laughed. "Okay, why do I need pants? I have at least an hour before Mom gets here with Nate, so waffle first, pants later." I hopped off the counter and grabbed my plate.

I took the butter and the syrup to the table with me and plopped in my chair.

"Do you want coffee?" he asked me.

"Yeah. Thanks." I slapped some butter on my waffle and took a bite. *Yum.*

That was a great start to a new week. I was really diggin' the normal life again.

Monday through Thursday was relatively quiet except for Tyler being a train wreck trying to make everything perfect for Rachel's big surprise. Finally, I was given the go-ahead and spoke with Rachel. Everything was set up for us to be at The London in Midtown at nine in the evening for the big engagement extravaganza. I received specific instructions that this was to be in "real time" and not "Jordie and Rachel time." Nine p.m. sharp it was.

*August 23rd*

*I've ridden my bike around that neighborhood every night this past week. I KNOW there's something. I feel obsessed. But you need something to be obsessed with, right? I just can't quite figure out what it is...yet.*

*August 30th*

*I walked up and down the block tonight. Back and forth—I blended in. It's amazing how many people wear Yankees caps and sunglasses at night. Suddenly, I got bits and pieces. Flashes of those boots. I saw them and someone's hands with blood on them. Jesus Christ, did I hurt someone? Did I help a murderer or something? No... not enough blood for that. But those hands. I CANT FUCKING EXPLAIN IT. I never thought that to get my memories back I'd have to lose my goddamned mind like this. I need a break, but I can't stop thinking about it. Any of it.*

*I should call Lena. Maybe get some. Did I really just say that? I guess so. Maybe a stress reliever is all I need to get focused again.*

I stared straight ahead and closed the journal.

*'Maybe I should get some'?*

I felt my stomach tighten up and my teeth clench.

*Quit being such a drama mamma. He didn't know you existed. And even when he didn't know, he knew. Keep reading.*

I opened the journal again and took a deep breath, holding it in for a few seconds before letting it out with a big gush of air and noise. At the same time, Nathan walked in the room and smiled at me.

"What are you smiling at, ya nut-job?" I asked with a grin.

"Just the fact that you thought you couldn't deal with knowing and now you're in here doing some light reading without me."

Nathan jumped on the bed, lay back against the pillows and motioned for me to come sit with him. He sat up against the headboard and I sat in between his legs, leaning my back on his chest. He rested his chin on my shoulder for a second and then kissed it.

*August 31st*

*I made plans with Lena for next week. I rented a room on a different floor. The folks will be back. I don't want to disappoint Mom by looking like a womanizer, but goddamn, I was willing to try anything at this point. Even no-strings-attached sex. I have no idea if that is even normal. Maybe I should ask Frank or Tyler.*

*September 3rd*

*I asked Frank if I was a no-strings-attached, one-night-stand kind of guy, or what... His response was "or what." Instead of answers, I'm ending up with more questions.*

# finding nathan

*Now I know I'm fucking mental. What kind of man has a hot chick rubbing all up on him, begging for it...and he says no? It was like a bad trip. At first, I was ok, I was into it. Alright, yeah, she's hot. I'm a guy... I got shot and can't remember anything, so I deserve a little, right? WRONG. The only thing that got fucked was my mind. One. Huge. Mindfuck. I was fine doing the over-the-clothes shit, but once her shirt came off and she straddled me, my brain hurt. I literally shook my head to try to shake it off...but I couldn't. The more she moved, the more flashed through my mind. Holy fuck, just thinking about it exhausts me. It was tolerable until she put her hands in my hair. Then it was like I was being haunted by my own memory. A voice— it was HER voice—repeating my name. "Nathan. Nathan. Nathan." I practically tossed Lena off me. I apologized and told her she had to go. The boots. The hands. The voice. They're all connected...but who is she?*

I closed the journal and realized I had a steady stream of tears running down my face. I felt like I was going to puke. I ripped Nathan's hands apart from around me, jumped out of the bed, and ran to the bathroom.

I was sweaty and clammy.

*What. The. Fuck. How much of the "over-the-clothes thing" did he do with her? She was a hot chick rubbing all up against him? Jordan, you stupid, stupid, stupid-ass. You knew this was coming.*

"Jordan? Unlock it," Nathan called through the door, but I made no attempt to move.

"Please?" he asked.

Still, I leaned against the vanity sink, wiping my tears.

"Now...," Nathan demanded.

*Fuck. He means business.*

I walked over and unlocked the door.

**78**

"If you *knew* there was something missing, someone important, something you were obsessing over, why would you do *that*?" I broke down.

I wasn't expecting that. I wasn't even sure how I felt about him knowing that was in there and thinking it was okay for me to read it. And with *her*? He knew how I felt about her. What's worse was she knew about me and never mentioned it. She wasn't one of those bitches that worried about other people's needs. If she thought telling him about me, Emma, and the baby would've benefitted her, she'd have been all over it.

*Another bitch. What is wrong with these women?*

"I'm not okay with *that*, Nathan," I sobbed. "I need to know if there is more of *that*? If so, I'm out. I'm not reading any more."

I wrapped my arms around my stomach and bent over, crying harder. Silently, but harder.

"No more. That was the last time I touched anyone," Nathan answered.

I stood up, wiped my tears, and sniffled.

"That broke my heart, Nathan."

I started to cry again but held it back a bit. If I hadn't, I would have gone into full-on Oprah cry, and I wasn't having that shit.

Nathan pushed the hair away from my face and hugged me.

"Mine too, baby. I didn't even know you existed, yet I was heartbroken and disgusted with myself." He kissed the top of my head, then picked me up so I could sit on the counter.

"I love you that much, Jordan. I'm so sorry."

He leaned in and kissed me. Not his I-wanna-eat-your-face-and-hump-you-until-you-can't-stand kind of kiss, either. It was a sweet, long and apologetic kiss.

"You're forgiven." I sniffled and wrapped my legs around him.

Blue eyes to green, we searched each other's hearts.

"I can't forgive myself that quickly; I sure as hell don't expect you to forgive me that quickly," Nathan joked and rested his forehead against mine.

"I won't apologize for how I feel, but I can forgive what happened. I'll just keep telling myself you were out of your mind." I grinned.

"This is why I wanted to do this with you. Why I wanted you to read this," Nathan said.

"So we would fight and make up?" I leaned in and kissed him.

"No. I didn't want any secrets between us. I didn't want to feel like I was hiding it from you. I wanted you to know so we could move past it together. I couldn't forgive myself without knowing you forgave me," he confessed.

"Well, go easy on yourself. We'll get through this," I said as I pulled my shirt over my head.

"Oh yeah, and however will we manage that?" he asked with his gorgeous lazy grin that made me want to bite his lip and do dirty, dirty things to him.

"Lots and lots of this." I pulled him as close as possible and my hands were in his hair a second later. I forgave him in my own special way—over and over—that night.

# chapter *fourteen*

I RAN AROUND ALL day Friday. Nathan had gone with Tyler to pick up his mom and siblings at the airport and get them settled. I had to keep Rachel busy, so Fiona and I met her at the bar. I was happy, because it meant I got to spend a good part of the day with my little handsome man before he went to his GiGi's for the weekend. Emma was going to Kelly's after school, so we had a few hours before I had to be back to get her ready to go, and my sister wasn't good with the whole waiting thing.

We went to a few shops until Rachel and I picked out the perfect dress for our Girls' Night Out dinner. I just had to get her there at nine and all would be right with the world.

When we pulled up to her place, I hugged her and handed her the dress bag.

"Such a hot dress," I said.

"Too bad you're the only one that's going to see it." She sulked.

"Just leave it on for when he gets home." I tried to cheer her up.

"Yeah. I guess." She pulled her keys out of her purse.

"Rach, I promise you, he isn't steppin' out on you. I'll be here at eight-forty. Got it? We cannot be late. We'll lose the reservation. Chin up until then. No frowny faces allowed." I reached over and pushed her cheeks up into a smile like putty in my hands, but she stood there deadpan.

"You're an asshole," she said through me holding her lips up.

I busted out laughing and let go when I felt her mouth tighten into a smile.

"There we go. Much better." I sat back in the driver's seat.

She flipped me the finger and gave me the international duck-face of fuck-off.

"Okay, biotch. See you later. Bye, Fiona. It was nice to see you, and thank you for that seminar on ovulation and hormones. I'll pick up my pamphlets at the door," she said to Nathan's mom with a smile and a humorous eye roll.

"Yeah, yeah, smart-ass," Fiona replied as she climbed out of the back to get into the front seat. "Goodbye. Go. Behave and have fun tonight." She shooed Rachel off.

"Bye, Rach, see you in a few hours." I pulled off.

Nathan left at six to pick up Tyler and his family. They had to stop by the jewelry store to pick up the ring because Tyler had nowhere safe to hide it. Rachel had her hands all over the place—the bar, their apartment, our place—nothing was safe. She was always digging through something of mine.

When I finished my hair, I changed into my just-above-the-knee-length tulle-bottom black dress with capped sleeves and a black sequin top, and I slipped on my very first pair of Valentino Garavani's, fresh off the plane from Paris, France this afternoon. I was ashamed of myself for spending what I had on them. I could get twenty pairs of boots for what I spent on this one pair of shoes, but it was for a special occasion, so I splurged.

As I walked down the hallway, I laughed at the clickety-clack sound they made. I wasn't used to hearing that sound from underneath me. I also wasn't used to being so tall. I was holding my sapphire necklace in one hand and my black matching clutch in the other. When I got to the living room, Frank was sitting on the couch, reading a newspaper.

"They still make them things?" I joked about his newspaper.

"Looks that way. I know, I was surprised as well." He laughed as he folded it up and put it on the table.

"Look at you. You look beautiful, Jordan." He reached for my hand and gave me a twirl.

"Thank you, sir." I curtsied. "Could I trouble you to put this on me, please?"

I held out my hand and showed him my necklace. He took it from me and I moved my hair out of the way.

"Ready to go?" Frank asked.

"Ready."

We arrived at The London at nine sharp, just like I was instructed. When Frank took the ticket from the valet, Rachel gave me a what-the-fuck look.

"The pitbull is joining us for our girls' night out?" she snorted.

"Ha!" I busted out and looked back at Frank.

"I'm not a pitbull," he replied in a sing-song voice through a fake smile.

"No, you're a bat with that fucking hearing," Rachel mumbled and we all laughed.

I had no idea where they were, so when the host led us through the main dining area, I made sure I stayed in front of Rachel; I didn't want her to see everyone and ruin the surprise. As we neared the back, I saw a semi-private area.

"Jesus Christ, where are we sitting? In the kitchen, buddy?" Rachel blurted out.

I smacked her with my clutch by waving my arm behind me.

"Be nice, Rachel," I hissed.

Just as we got to the entrance of the room, I stepped to the side so she could walk in first. I looked in and saw my gorgeous husband in that Gucci suit that makes me drippy in all the right places.

Rachel blurted out, "What, are we getting our own—"

She stopped dead in her tracks when she realized who was in the room.

"What...the...hell? It isn't my birthday. Is it?" She looked at me, dumbfounded.

All I could do was laugh, because it was a rare thing to see Rachel speechless. It was like seeing a unicorn shitting another unicorn that was shitting a rainbow.

When the lights dimmed, I motioned for her to look across the room where Tyler was sitting on a stool upon a makeshift stage area. There was a slideshow of pictures running on the wall behind him.

Nathan walked over and stood next to me. I started to get all teary-eyed when I saw Rachel's eyes fill up as she made her way to Tyler. He began to play his guitar and sing a song he wrote for her. Nathan slipped his arm around my waist and kissed my head.

"You look amazing," he whispered in my ear.

"You are one hot piece of ass, Mr. Harper, and I can't wait to take that suit off of you," I whispered back.

"Really, now. I may have some fun myself taking that dress off of you... with my teeth." He ran his hand over my hips and ass. I sucked in a huge breath and held it because his hand was so close to the hem of my dress.

"You have any idea how easily my hand could disappear up here? Nobody would be the wiser with all this fluffy stuff to work under." He positioned me so I was standing in front of him as he hugged me from behind.

I'm pretty sure it was to hide what was happening inside his pants at that moment. I dropped my clutch on purpose, bent over to pick it up, and when I rubbed against him, he let out a hushed groan.

I took a tiny step away from him so the party in his pants would settle down before the lights got turned back up. He moved my hair to the side and kissed my neck.

"Just you wait," his lips pressed against the skin right below my ear.

I just concentrated on breathing so I wouldn't pass out from all the blood rushing to one place...and it wasn't my head. I felt his phone vibrate as the lights began to come back on and he pulled it out of his pocket. He stifled a laugh.

I looked back at him in question and he turned his phone so I could see what it said.

Frank: Wildly inappropriate behavior at an engagement party, FYI.

We laughed and made our way over to Rachel and Tyler, and Nathan pulled me tight against his side. Tyler was on his knee in front of Rachel.

"Wanna make an honest man out of me?" He grinned up at her, and she knelt down with him and said yes. Well, she cried yes.

As soon as they finished, she turned and threw her arms around me.

"Is this payback, you effin' bitch, for the week I had to keep my mouth shut about your engagement?" She laughed.

"Oh yeah, I forgot about all that. Yep, consider us even. I'm so happy for you," I gushed.

"Alright, tone it down. No need to get all hormonal on me now." She busted out laughing.

"When did we decide to grow up, Jordan?" Rachel asked me, dead serious.

"I don't think we had any say in this." I smiled. "It was just time, I guess." I hugged her before she walked away.

"Wanna go find a utility closet or something?" I turned to Nathan who was standing behind me again.

"I thought you'd never ask." He smiled and escorted me out of the room.

We looked all over that place, but there was not one room private enough for a quickie, and I don't do bathrooms. *Yuck.* I noticed the line of cars out the front window and I had an idea.

"Is your car service still out there?" I grinned mischievously at him.

"You're brilliant," he said as he led the way.

When we got out front, Nathan looked for the driver. I looked in the opposite direction and noticed someone getting out of an SUV.

"That bitch is *here?*" I said a little too loudly, gaining the attention of quite a few people in close proximity to me, including Nathan.

"Who?" he asked.

"Lena." I pulled Nathan with me as I walked away.

"Talk about a cock-block," Nathan muttered under his breath.

As we approached the door to go back inside, Lena put some pep in her step to catch up with us. I prayed she didn't say anything to set me off. I already wanted to rip off her head and feed it to her ass for breakfast. After all, she did know all about me when she tried seducing Nathan.

*Bigger person, Jordan... Be the bigger person.* I chose not to fight that battle.

"Jordie? Nate? What a coincidence bumping into you guys here," Lena said just as we almost slipped past her.

*God dammit.*

"Sorry, can't talk, need to get back inside, nice to see you," I said in one swift sentence.

"Jordie, could I steal you for a second? I'd really like to clear something up with you." She put on one hell of a dog and pony show when people were watching.

"Nathan, go say goodbye to everyone. Let them know I'm not feeling well, and grab my jacket, please." I asked Nathan before he kissed my forehead and quietly asked if I was okay. I nodded and let his hand go.

"Tell Rachel I'll call her tomorrow," I told him and then turned to Lena.

"What can I do for you, Lena?"

As if my less-than-enthusiastic tone wasn't evidence enough, my lack of posture and eye contact should have gotten the message across loud and clear. I didn't want any part of this.

"Jordie, I know the things that you hear must really get to you, but I want you to know that I would never, ever go after a married man." She put her hand on mine and came across like she was throwing me a sympathetic pity party with her eyes; it made me snap.

"Well, that's reassuring, being that you were like a bitch in heat the second you thought you had a chance with Nathan. Even knowing I was pregnant. It's a good thing I know *my husband* has no reason to stray. He fought pretty damn hard to find me, so I'm pretty sure he isn't going anywhere—not that I need to tell you that, right? You'd *never* go after someone's husband," I smiled sweetly and spoke softly.

It's more threatening when you whisper and have a calm, beady-eye stare going on. That's right. I busted out the ol' crazy eyes trick. Besides, the paps were everywhere now so to them we were just having a friendly conversation.

"Lena, Jordie, can we get a pic of you two?" one of the paps asked.

"Well, you sure can." I smiled animatedly and looked at Lena. "Right, friend?"

I pulled her in close to me with my arm around her shoulder and smiled for the cameras.

"Right, friend," she answered through her clenched teeth.

Nathan walked out of the restaurant with Frank, Rachel and Tyler in tow. The four of them stood frozen with amused looks on their faces. Before Lena and I parted ways, I laid on the theatrics by embracing her in a long sisterly hug and lots of smiles. Nathan and I said our goodbyes and hopped in the limo.

# chapter *fifteen*

October 3rd

That night with Lena caused something in my brain to snap. I don't give a shit what happened to me in the past. All I can think about is HER. The Voice with the Boots is what I've been calling her.

Night after night, I ride my bike out to the East Village and watch everyone go by. Even the sky holds some sort of importance in the grand scheme of it all, but I can't put it together. So I wander.

October 21st

Yesterday I got there early, so I took a seat on a bench. It was dusk, so I could still see faces. Around 5, I noticed Tyler and Rachel walking across the street. I stood to call them but I saw they had a little girl with them. I walked a short distance behind them on the opposite side of the street. When I saw the bar, I assumed it was where Rachel works. I know she's a bartender; I just don't know where. But they didn't go to the bar. They stopped at the building next to it. I looked up and saw lights on. They went inside. I looked higher...to the sky above that building... It sucker punched me. I KNOW that sky.

October 23rd

I stayed in and watched TV all day. Flipping through the channels, I came across an older movie with Melissa Joan Hart and the guy from Entourage—Grenier. I stayed on it for a few seconds because Ali Larter looked amazing with red hair, but then a song began playing and the hair on my neck stood up. I KNEW the song. My heart broke... It actually drew my body inward. GODDAMN IT, WHY CAN'T I REMEMBER ANY OF THIS??? WHAT AM I DOING WRONG? I cried alone...on the couch of the hotel...with a bag of Cheetos. I just cried.

"I'll never be able to watch you eat Cheetos again." I closed the journal with a quick snap and put it on my nightstand.

"Well, I hope you never watch me eat anything…ever, honestly. That's sort of strange." We laughed together, then he continued. "Yeah, that was a rough night for me. You have no idea how frustrating it is to want something so badly and not even know what it is."

He ran his hand over my stomach.

*Stop that, you're making me tingle.*

"It's that feeling when the answer is riiiight there on the tip of your tongue but never evolves into an answer." He rolled onto his side. He had one arm across his chest with his hand tucked under the other arm. He was still rubbing my stomach and his facial expression read concentration.

"You okay?" I asked, but he was silent.

"Seriously, Nathan. What is it?"

"I was just thinking about something Lena said to me that night. It didn't make any sense then, but it does now. Wow, she's such a bitch," he said with a sneer.

"Not exactly who I'd like to hear you're thinking about, but okay, I'll play. What'd she say?" I asked sarcastically.

"She said it was ironic that I was the one throwing her out, because she was willing to accept me all fucked up, just the way I was. Even if I got my memory back and she lost me, she'd still be willing to take that chance just to be with me. Unlike those who have the chance to claim what's theirs but instead choose not to. I get it now. She meant you."

"Talk about fixated." I scoffed.

"Isn't it amazing that even though I had the memory of an Alzheimer's patient, I still knew it was wrong? That she wasn't you. You were missing." He propped himself up and gave the side of my panties a snap.

"Yeah, that's some Nicolas Sparks' *The Notebook* shit right there," I said, clearly not enjoying the thought of that intimate incident.

He leaned over and kissed my stomach.

*Ooh my, ohh my...*

As he kissed and touched me, he made his way to where he hovered over me between my legs.

"You...know...I..." *Well, fuck. I can't think.*

"You what?" he asked between his kisses that became more and more sensual with each one.

"I... I don't know."

I gave up, exasperated, and grabbed his hair with both hands. He let out one of his panty-dropping growls and I was done. I forgot about all of it. All I could feel was his breath against my skin and his tongue never leaving my body as he tugged my panties off. His kisses trailed down and stopped right before his final destination. Then he wrapped his arms under my knees, grabbed the top of my thighs, and yanked me down so I went from leaning against the headboard to flat on my back. His hand was back on my stomach as he made his way up my shirt, while his mouth made its way down. It was going to be one of those amazing I-see-colors-and-fireworks kinds of nights.

I gently lifted his hand off my chest and started to wriggle out from under him. He mumbled a little bit and rolled over, freeing me from my own personal sauna. I slipped on my shirt and went to get a drink. When I came back in, I stood at the floor-to-ceiling window and looked out over the city. I loved the privacy glass option. We could always see out but nobody could see in. Even at a quarter to three in the morning, it was bustling out there.

I heard rustling in the sheets but paid no mind to it until I felt him against me from behind. He slid his hands around and rubbed back and forth over my rib cage, massaging me. I raised my arm over my head so I could touch his hair. He found the spot in the crook of my neck and walked us to the window.

*Score… Window sex. Yesss.*

The thought alone made my legs weak. Knowing all that was keeping the entire Upper East Side from seeing us was some window tint pretty much made me shameless.

Once we were at the window, he pressed up against me as his hand found his way down to me. The window was cold and being up against it so hard made every nerve tingle.

*He hasn't even touched you yet… Jesus Christ, this man.*

It didn't matter that he was simply groping me. That did it for me—*he* did it for me. The thought of Nathan's hands touching every inch of my skin, biting me playfully and growling just the right things in my ear, was all I needed. The man was a bucket of sex appeal and he belonged to me.

He slipped two fingers in and moved his thumb just right… Once… Twice… *Fuck… Game over.* I came apart… I mean really *came* apart. I must have been talking some pretty dirty shit because Nathan let loose. Now don't get me wrong, he's always a beast in bed. It never mattered if we took our time, fucked like bunnies, or just teased each other; it had always been something special, different, exciting. But when he got like this—when I could tell he wasn't holding back at all—I could expect a few bruises in the morning on the both of us.

He shoved his hand into the hair at the nape of my neck and held it so tightly and closely that I couldn't really move. He pulled me back away from the window and bent me over.

"Put both hands on the glass," he demanded. "Do you even know how much you mean to me?" he asked as he ran his fingers lightly up and down my back, teasing every curve of my body. I couldn't answer him. Shit, I couldn't complete a thought let alone string any words together.

"Do you?" He stopped touching me and nudged into me from behind, hard, pushing me forward a bit.

"I think... I think I do," I answered, slightly dazed.

*Can't we discuss this later? Oh, god. He's going to end up fucking me stupid.*

He nudged me again. "This is mine."

He reached around and pulled me against him. He may as well have whipped out a flag and claimed me, he was so rough.

"Ye...yes...all...yours. Nathan, *please, baby,* do something before I fucking explode," I begged and pushed against him harder.

That's all it took—me asking him. His long fingers explored me for a few moments until he was rubbing himself slowly against me.

"Oh my god, Nathan, *please,*" I screamed out, partly in pure fucking pleasure and partly because I needed him to be inside me.

He grabbed my hips and yanked me up so hard that my feet left the ground for a moment and did more than *something* to me.

*I was wrong... He was going to fuck me into a coma. One floor up from fucking me stupid... It's coming.*

I lost all control and any sense of reality. With that, my arms became weak. He stopped, pulled me up, and walked me to the chaise.

"Nathan... I have no strength... Two already... I'm...," I peeped out, dropping my head onto the lounger as we knelt down in front of it.

"You want to stop?" He leaned forward, pushed the hair off my face and kissed my neck.

"No." I shook my head.

"Just don't expect any reverse cowboy action from me." I let out a small laugh.

He kissed my shoulder and stood up, helping me up with him. He walked us over to the bed and told me to lie down. I did what I was told and waited as he climbed over me.

My god, I was a big drippy ball of sexual tension and he knew exactly what to do to relieve me.

He was rough and sweet at the same time. Then boom, just like that, he disproved another one of my "that shit doesn't happen in real life" theories.

"I want to feel you come apart around me," he said in my ear.

He begged and I lost it. He never took his eyes off me. I could feel them burn through me, and it wasn't until I was done that he let go.

I slept in Saturday morning. I was so fantastically sore that when I yelped as I stretched and got out of bed, I smiled. I could hear Nathan talking to someone, so I decided to hop in the shower and let the hot water work over some of those achy muscles I had. I hit the preheat shower button and started to brush my teeth. I hopped in and just let the water wash over me for a good five or ten minutes. The other plus side to the new place: the water never turned cold.

After my ridiculously long shower, I wrapped a towel around my head, dried off, and threw on my favorite pair of yoga pants and one of my old sweatshirts. It'd been a while since I wore anything dressed down like this.

The forecast was calling for snow and the sky looked about right for it. I planned to spend the day watching TV with three of my four favorite men: Nathan, Ben and Jerry. When I headed down the hallway, I heard Nathan still talking. When I passed by, I realized the door was almost all the way shut so I didn't stop. I figured he needed to be alone.

I grabbed some Chunky Monkey out of the freezer and my favorite blanket off the couch and made myself comfortable. It was the first time using the TV in the new place, so it took me a minute to figure out how to turn it on. Once I did, I was flipping through five hundred channels of crap. I turned E! on and kept up with the Kardashians for like three seconds before the mom made me want to gouge my own eyes out with a rusty nail. I have to admit that I love Khloe though. I totally fangirled when Nathan introduced us at a party in LA. I have that picture filed under *Holy shit, did that just happen?*I began flipping through the channels again when I stopped at *Old Yeller*. I put down the remote and dug into my ice cream. Just as the end of the movie was playing, my phone rang; it was Emma. I was a sobbing mess when I answered the phone on speaker. I wasn't putting Ben or Jerry down.

"Hey, sweetie." I sniffled when I answered.

"Hi, Mom. What's wrong? You okay?" She'd picked up on my tone immediately.

"Yeah, baby, I'm fine. I just watched *Old Yeller*," I explained.

"Oh, Christ, not Old Yeller. Who let you watch that, Jordan?" I heard Kelly chime in from the background. I guessed I was on speaker as well.

"Shut up, Kel," I yelled back at her and started sobbing again.

"Mom, it's okay. I promise you, they did what was best for *Ol' Yeller*," Emma assured me.

*When did this kid start growing up?*

"Wow, I step away for an hour, and right away you fall apart. You know it's bad when a ten-year-old is teaching her mother life lessons," Nathan said as he walked in the living room and sat down next to me. "Hi, Em," he added.

"Hey, Nathan."

"I just wanted to let you know that Aunt Kelly said that if it snows there, she isn't bringing me home until Tuesday," she relayed.

"Okay. I'd rather you guys stay put if it gets bad out. No driving—tell her. Walk up to the store if you need something. It's like a half a block away."

"Yes, Mom. Love you. Talk to ya later. Love you, too, Nathan," Emma said before hanging up.

"Well, I love you too." I stared at my phone before tossing it on the couch pillow.

"She probably couldn't handle all the weepiness that's happening over here," Nathan said, stifling his laugh.

"Fuck off, Nathan." I sniffled playfully as I sat up. I pretended to wipe my nose across my sleeve and said, "Gimme a kiss," while making a snot-nosed fish-face.

"I will. I'll kiss that mouth—I don't care what you have all over it." He leaned in and I pushed him away playfully.

"Ew, noooo, you're gross!" I laughed as he kept coming at me.

"I'll take your lips any way I can get them, sugar." He tackled me and we fell to the floor. I laughed until I nearly peed in my pants.

Nathan just watched me with a smile on his face.

# chapter
## *sixteen*

NATHAN WANTED TO TAKE a nap, since he pretty much stayed awake after the three a.m. sexapalooza. Something was troubling him. I thought it might be work. He was rather vehement when he mentioned not acting anymore. Maybe the directing or producing gig didn't come through and he's upset about that. I didn't care what he did as long as we were happy and could take care of our kids. We lay down together and he fell out almost immediately.

I ran my fingers through his hair as I watched him breathe. He had me in a full-on bear hug, so I could only move my arms from the elbows down. I was sure I looked comical trying to pick up his journal. I slid myself up carefully, so I didn't wake him, and adjusted myself to get comfortable.

"Let's see what you were thinking next, Mister Harper," I said with a sigh and opened the journal.

*October 31st*

*It's Halloween night, and I'm sitting on the bench. I've watched this building every single night for the last few* nights but seen nobody come in or out—no one but Rachel and Tyler going in with the little girl. I haven't talked to Tyler much since the whole man-whoring comment... Why am I lying? I haven't talked to anyone, really—aside from my parents. Not even Frank. He went home to LA for a few weeks, but he'll be back tomorrow.

Things with Mom are much better. She doesn't understand why I have to go out on my bike for hours every night...but she said if it helps clear my head, she understands. I know she worries.

HOLY SHIT. For the first time in ten days, I've seen someone other than the three of them come or go. A woman... I couldn't make out her face or anything. She's with the same kid. She looks almost as tall as the small woman, until she jumps off the bottom step, dressed in a costume. Looks like they're waiting for someone. The woman is pregnant.

They must all been going trick-or-treating together. I heard the kid yell out Frank's name and I looked up just in time to see him pick up the kid and hug her. Then he hugged the pregnant girl and gave her a kiss on the cheek. That made my blood boil... Why would he lie to me about when he'd be back? But what really pushed me over the edge was when Mom and Dad got out of Frank's car.

November 1st

I'm pretty sure I got so angry I blacked out.

The last thing I remember was standing up and pacing back and forth, back and forth. I remember hearing the woman laugh and it echoed in my mind. I knew it matched The Voice with the Boots. I wondered why everyone I cared about was over there. Did I miss a text or a call with an invite? No. They're hiding something. I remember I stopped pacing and stopped thinking. I instinctively began to walk over and find out what the fuck was going on, but when I turned, I bumped right into Frank. That's the last thing I remember...but at least I have a lot more info now. I know everyone is in on it, like they're hiding my happiness. I'm done. Done with all of them. If they want to shut me out, I can do the same to them.

December 1st

Not much to report, I guess. I do everything on my own these days. I go to the studio alone, I eat alone, and I ride around alone. The tabloids reported that I cracked and entered a mental rehab facility, yet others have me shacked up with Lena in our "love nest."

I look like I should be in an episode of Duck Dynasty. I haven't shaved in a month... Eh, nobody recognizes me, so I'm good with that. Every night, I sit. Alone. Ok, well, I'm embellishing a bit. I'm not alone all the time. I've gotten to know a few of the elderly people who live on that side of the block. I like them because to them I'm just some lonely kid who hangs out on a street bench. They don't know I'm Nate Harper.

Edna lives two buildings down from my bench. She's what they refer to as a snowbird. Normally, she'd be in Florida right now, but her husband is stuck at the Veteran's retirement rehab because they can't afford a full-time nurse. I saw her struggling to get her trash out one night about three weeks ago. I've helped her and the woman in the apartment next to her out a few times with the trash since then. They've come out and chatted me up quite a bit on the milder nights. Edna told me about her husband two nights ago when she asked if I would mind coming inside to shut off a water valve that was leaking

**98**

in her bathroom. She didn't have the strength.

When I walked into her place, the first thing I noticed were all the pictures on the wall. I could feel it stirring in the void, creeping its way through my bones. It was like the pizza place deja vu: one mindfuck coming up. DING. So many pictures of them together, her husband in uniform, the American flag, a Purple fucking Heart, and he was shoved into some second-rate home care facility because they didn't have enough money? This was his home. I quickly made a mental note of his name because by that time I was struggling to keep my shit together. I knew I might come unhinged after I shut off the valve, so I needed to get the hell out of there. When I walked back out of the bathroom, it was as if I was standing in a different living room. Pictures on a wall... A huge one in the back of the room, but I couldn't make out the faces... An American flag. It was spinning. I turned, and Edna asked if I was ok... The words "It was a long time ago" are all I hear. In that voice... In her voice.

I let out a huge gust of air when I finished that entry, because I didn't even realize I had been holding my breath.

"Oh, Nathan, I'm so sorry you had to go through all that," I whispered while I played with his hair and watched him sleep for a few minutes before I started packing him up for Vancouver. His phone kept vibrating, so I went to click it off when I saw a text from Lena: All set for Vancouver? I'll be on the one o'clock out.

*You'll be on what? My stomach got that nervous sick feeling. Why didn't he tell me Lena was going to Vancouver?*

I opened up the text and there was one from last night. It really set me off.

Lena: You look hot in that suit.

About ten minutes later, Nathan replied.

Nathan: Stop it, Lena.

*Holy shit, I'm going to lose it.*

Lena: Come get your jacket

Nathan: If my keys weren't in it, I'd leave it behind.

Lena: You'll have to find them first.

Nathan: That's ok. Keep them. I'll get the locks changed.

Lena: Speaking of changing your locks...you should change your passwords too.

Almost immediately, Nathan replied.

Nathan: What passwords? And why would I need to change them, Lena?

Lena: Oh, Nathan, get your head out of the clouds. Come back to earth. And tell your wife's bitch BFF if she calls me an insufferable cow again I'll show her how insufferable I can be. See ya soon!

"Son of a bitch," I muttered.

*All right, Jordan. You can go in there and start going off like a crazy lady, or you can ask questions and find out what the fuck is actually going on.*

*One crazy lady, comin' right up.*

I had nothing to say to Lena that wouldn't come across as incriminating in court, so I decided to take it to my husband.

"What the fuck is this shit, Nathan?" I stomped in our room and threw the phone at his still-sleeping head.

*Maybe that was a bad idea... No more head trauma.*

"Ow! What the fuck, Jordan? What did you do that for? Are you serious right now?" He came back at me.

"Whatever. What is this shit about Lena going to Vancouver and how you look hot in that suit?" My voice got louder and louder with every word.

"Jesus Christ, Jordie." Nathan rubbed his face and got out of bed.

"I told her to knock it off. You saw her at The London last night. I tried to avoid her. Then she texted me. I didn't want to upset you with it. Then I witnessed the whole pissing contest you two had. That must have been emotionally draining enough for you," he said in an annoyed tone.

"Was that fucking sarcasm? A *pissing contest*, Nathan? Really? She's chasing my husband around and it's a pissing contest on my part? And what is this 'come back to earth' bullshit? You two have some sort of secret sexy talk from when you were chasing her hot ass?" I yelled, gesturing violently with my hands. I *am* Italian, after all.

"Jordan…I thought you understood that there are women—lots and lots of them—and even some men that want what you have: *me*. What does it matter when all I want is you?" He stood up and shouted at me.

Yeah, his frustration level had capped out. He was going to lose his cool. We rarely fought, and even when we did, it would last five minutes and then all was forgiven. But this shit, hell no. This was serious business and I wanted it handled.

"Why didn't you tell me she was going then? Huh?" I stood solid with my hands on my hips, waiting for an answer.

He rubbed his face again and sat on the edge of the bed with his elbows on his knees. He took a deep breath and ran his hands through his hair, then exhaled and looked up at me.

"I didn't know until her agent caught me on the way out of the party last night. He said Lena was Victoria's replacement because she got pregnant and can't shoot now," he explained.

"And you failed to tell me all this, why?" I asked in a calmer voice.

"Because I didn't want to upset you for no reason. I planned to let the studio know if she ends up being right for the part, I'll have to withdraw from the project. I planned to let them know it's not anything personal, but more of a creative style difference. Which, of course, would be a lie, but 'I hate the bitch' doesn't really work in the big bad world of responsibility."

"Saving me once again, I see. Stop. I'd much rather just know what's going on. This way, when the headlines read that we're the second generation Jennifer Aniston and Brad Pitt, I'm prepared and not blindsided," I snapped back at him.

"Oh my fucking god, you frustrate me. And don't give me the 'saving me' bullshit. Pot meet kettle, you'd say, no?" He pulled at his hair with both hands.

"I'm done. I need some air. There's your bag. I'll see ya when you get home. And don't think I didn't notice you avoided my question about the 'come back to earth' bullshit. Yeah. Nice. Real nice." I stomped out of the bedroom and down the hall, grabbed my scarf, jacket, gloves, and boots from the entrance closet and headed down to the street. It was starting to snow.

*Fucking global warming and shit. Seventy-one and Margaritas on Tuesday, twenty-nine and blizzard-like conditions on Saturday. Makeup your mind, bitch.*

I walked the East Side for a few hours. I tried calling Rachel a couple of times, but it went right to voicemail. I decided to stop at my favorite Mexican place, Blockhead's, so I grabbed a cab and hit the one over in Midtown East.

I was kind of glad Rachel didn't answer. She just got engaged and I don't want to be all Debbie Downer on her happy time. I called my sister and talked to her while I ate. She was always my voice of reason. She never told me how to live my life but she always knew what to say when things weren't going so great, or I was acting like a "Jordhole." Yes, that stands for a Jordie-asshole.

"Jordan, he was trying to *not* get you all worked up. You're the asshole for even going the Jenn and Brad route. Lena is no Angelina, that's fo' sho, Then again, you're no Jennifer Aniston, either." Kelly teased me.

I couldn't help but laugh.

"Maybe I overreacted a bit. Nathan did mention quitting the on-screen side of the business. He wants to try some new things. Maybe that was his way of letting me know something wasn't right," I admitted to her.

"You? Overreact? That's doubtful, Jords." She was such a sarcastic twat sometimes.

"Fuck off." I laughed.

"And as far as the secret sexy code talk, I think it's safe to say getting your head out of the clouds isn't very sexy at all." She laughed

"Come back to earth. She said *come back to earth...get your head out of the clouds…"*

And then it clicked. *In the clouds. On the cloud. ON the fucking cloud.*

"Shit, Kelly, I figured it out. I gotta go. I'll explain later. Love ya. Doubt it. Bye," I said before I cut off the call.

"Love you more! Doubt it, bye," she said at the same time as me.

I texted Nathan right away.

*Nathan. Back on earth, out of the clouds. Change your passwords? ON THE CLOUD? Please tell me it isn't possible, Nathan. Please tell me she didn't have our account hacked into.*

He didn't answer me. I had to get out of there and back home to find out. My phone was nearly dead; even if he called back or texted, I wouldn't know. *Fuck, I told you to erase that shit, Nathan.*

As I was digging for my wallet, I got a text from Frank demanding to know where I was, and then my phone died.

This day was getting more and more frustrating by the minute. I paid and left.

# chapter *seventeen*

I CAUGHT A CAB back to my side of town and got out over by the Ritz. I stopped in a coffee shop to use the restroom and grab a cup coffee. When I got out of the coffee shop, there were a few paparazzi taking pictures of me. I put my head down and tried to ignore their lame questions. Then one of them asked if I was worried about Nathan and Lena working together on this project.

*Wrong question, buddy.*

I stopped walking and turned to him.

"*Why* would I be worried?" I asked less than politely.

I guessed he didn't expect my hostility, because he looked shocked. That was my fault. I was always so nice to them. I thought they were all respectful like Todd was. I was so wrong. I used to think if I gave them what they wanted, they'd back off. But no…they just came back begging for more scraps, biting the hand that feeds them. Today, I'd be doing the biting.

"Well, because of their history," he stated simply.

My temper flared. I threw my coffee at his legs and knocked his camera out of his hands in a one-two fluid motion. Then…I started swinging. Not like

Mike Tyson swinging, more like Ralphie from a Christmas Story swinging. Flailing out of control, cursing, and crying as I just swung at this guy. Yep... I cracked. I heard someone yell "Stop," and I was pulled back. "If you can't control yourself, I'm going to have to cuff you and—"

"And what? You gonna throw me on your back and toss me in jail? I'm the fucking victim here." I spat out at the police officer, not thinking.

*And yup...that's exactly what he did.*

He handcuffed me and stood by me until a squad car could come and pick me up. Luckily, the jerkoff I took a few swings at didn't want to press any charges. Most men would never stand up in court and confess a woman beat on them. So, his ego saved my ass this time.

I began sobbing again and started to shiver.

"Would you like a blanket, Mrs. Harper?" The officer who had me all shackled up asked.

"No, I'm okay. Thanks. Besides, I've heard it's cold in cell block D; I'm prepping for my stay," I joked lamely.

"Nah, you're not going to jail, just a holding cell for a bit." He winked and grinned. "Please, can you take these off?" I asked.

"When the guy whose ass you were kicking leaves, I'll spring ya."

*Hallelujah.*

I heard my name called out from a distance. I could see two heads bobbing through the now dissipating crowd. Once the circle of rubberneckers spread out a bit, I could see it was Nathan and Frank.

I blew my hair out of my face. *Lovely, just what I need. Nathan and Frank seeing me in handcuffs.*

"Jordan, baby, are you okay? Jesus Christ," he said in a panic as he ran his hands all over my face and hair, and then threw me into his chest with a bear hug. I couldn't do anything but stand there like a stick of celery because I was still a cuffed like a criminal.

"Officer, is she under arrest?" Frank asked.

"No, sir," the officer answered as he put a phone in a plastic bag and sealed it.

"What's up with the phone?" I asked.

"Evidence," he answered.

I nodded and worried I'd be going to court after all if they had me assaulting this guy on video. *Damn technology. I knew it was trouble.*

"So, what's with the cuffs?" Nathan snapped.

"She was swinging at a paparazzo. I had to restrain her somehow," the officer answered Nathan.

"And somehow she's in trouble? Remove the cuffs, please?" Frank asked.

"As long as Layla Ali over here keeps her hands to herself," the officer said and spun me around.

"Easy," Nathan demanded.

"Easy? Okay, pal. You should be tellin' her that." He undid the cuffs and I immediately started rubbing my wrists.

"I'm so sorry, Nathan." I hugged him and sobbed.

"Well, that's all I need. I have your statement, Mrs. Harper. The precinct will call if they need anything else from you." My personal cop handed me a piece of paper with the incident report number on it in case I needed it.

"Wait, how did you even know what was happening?" I asked, confused.

"Rachel called. Said you were involved in something at the park and Isobel texted her a video someone sent Todd.

"Who *does* that?" I was disgusted.

"Well, there's a reason you were singled out, I think. Come on. I'll explain on the way." Nathan took off his jacket and threw it around me while Frank stopped a cab.

"So, after you left, Lena texted and said she had to talk to me. I ignored her because all I could really think about was you. I was worried sick…," he began as we got in the cab.

"He was," Frank agreed nonchalantly while looking out the window.

"But then this text came through." He handed me his phone.

I wanted to punch something but I couldn't, because the picture staring back at me from the phone sucker-punched me in the gut first.

"You… Where did you get this? I *knew* that's what she meant by the clouds. Dammit, Nathan." I panicked.

It was Nathan and me…in a still shot from one of our private videos.

"Someone posted it on the internet." He looked pale.

"Do they have all of it or just bits of it?" I asked. It didn't matter though. I knew deep down if they had that, they had everything.

"We don't know. My PR team was on it really fast, before *I* even knew about it. Naomi called—no shit—the moment after the pic was sent to me. They discovered that it was posted from an IP address never used before and at a completely different location than where it originated. A place that has free Wi-Fi. They're trying to locate the address. We can't get names without a court order though.

"Frank, can you get a court order for that stuff?" I asked the best man to know.

"Nope, internet porn holds no bearing on getting taken down. You're dumb enough to take any pic naked then you deserve to be exploited on the Internet," he answered in a matter-of-fact tone. "Just ask my daughter. Which reminds me, she won't be moving here," he muttered quickly, still looking out the window.

*Ummm okay, we can revisit that at a later date...*

"It's useless, anyway, Jordan. The account will be deleted but so many people have that pic by now that...," Frank stated the obvious.

"Well, it doesn't matter, right? We can just say it didn't really happen if they don't have all of the footage. There's a pic of you smacking me around online, but that isn't real either. We lived through that." I pointed out.

"But this is different. They stole this footage. This is invasion of privacy, right? Maybe even defamation of character. I mean, whoever did this is trying to make us look really bad," Nathan inquired.

"Don't pull a muscle," I said, patting his knee.

"Pull a muscle? Doing what?" Nathan looked lost.

"Reaching that far with those accusations." I stifled my humor but Frank just roared with laughter.

"Oh, kid, you're good." He laughed and fist bumped me.

*That* was what made me laugh.

We pulled up in front of our building, and Nathan paid the fare before we all got out. Once we were upstairs, Frank called Richard to come and investigate who hacked into the system and how they did it. Nathan's PR team is great, but Richard knows his shit and would get it done way faster.

That day was a doozy for us, both emotionally and physically. I couldn't wait to get in bed and FaceTime with my mother-in-law, because she'd been driving Nathan up a goddamn wall since she caught wind of what happened. Talk about embarrassing. Also, I wanted to see Nate. I already called Emma and let my sister know I made it home and that I was fine.

Nathan made the calls he needed to make to pull out of his trip to Vancouver.

Once I finished my to-do list, I got some stress-relieving lovin' from Nathan in the shower and then settled into bed.

"Are we having a naked night?" Nathan asked excitedly when he came back in the bedroom.

He stripped and hopped into bed. I immediately clung to him. He didn't even have a chance to get comfortable. I wrapped my arms, legs, and my entire body around him. I just let everything go. I knew he would never cheat on me. Our fight wasn't necessary but it's good to disagree or just bitch each other out every now and again. It keeps shit interesting and ventilated. Oh, and the making up part was the best part because it could get so intense. In that I-can't-move-my-limbs-after-that sort of way that stayed with you into the next day.

"Babe," I said.

"Yeah."

"I'm sorry I overreacted," I apologized.

"Don't be. Truth be told, I'd react the same exact way if the roles were reversed." He kissed my forehead.

"So, what's next? How do we find out who really posted the pic?" I wondered out loud.

"We wait for Frank and Richard to do their thing and go from there." He shrugged.

"Wonderful. A game of hurry up and wait. Meanwhile, we'll pray nothing else gets put out there," I said as I yawned.

"Pretty much," he responded.

"And thank you," he added.

"For what?"

"For not saying I told you so or getting angry because I didn't listen." He wiped the tears that formed in my eyes from my yawn.

"Don't thank me yet. There's always tomorrow. I was just too worried and exhausted to bring it up tonight," I teased and he kissed my forehead.

We must have fallen asleep, because Nathan and I were both out of it when we woke to the doorbell ringing over and over.

"What now?" Nathan complained as we rolled out of the bed, still half asleep.

We threw on some clothes and shuffled out of the bedroom to see who was at the door.

I glanced at the clock.

"It's only nine thirty?" I yawned. The doorbell rang again, and then one more time.

"All riiight already, damn," I yelled as I approached the door.

"Who is it?" I pressed the speaker.

"It's Leon from concierge, Mrs. Harper. I'm so sorry to bother you," he spoke through the door.

"What's going on now?" I complained as I opened it and gestured for him to come in.

"My apologies again, ma'am. The police are on their way, but I'm going to need you both downstairs to make a statement," he said, sounding rushed and out of breath.

"Whoa, slow down, a statement for what? I'm so lost here," I said and looked at Nathan for some help. He shrugged, looking just as confused as I was. Then Leon went into what happened with full force.

He was doing rounds earlier and noticed the key drawer was opened slightly. He knew he didn't leave it like that because of his OCD. So he called the police. He looked around a bit, but the dispatcher told him to stay put and wait for the officers.

"They caught the two guys and are downstairs in the lobby." He finished just as he ran out of air. *Amazing. How the hell did he do that?*

"Alright, that's great and all, but what the hell does that have to do with us?" Nathan's annoyed tone cut through my spaced-out thoughts of Leon's ability to talk that fast.

"Oh, right. Sorry." He slapped his forehead.

"The cops said it had to do with you and to come get you," he added, gesturing with his hands to indicate he didn't know any more. He looked concerned as he went to leave.

I thanked him and asked him to let the officers know we would be right down. When I turned to Nathan, he looked aggravated.

"Does it *ever* end?" he asked out loud—to himself, I'm assuming—as he walked down the hallway towards the bedroom. A few seconds later, he showed back up with pants on and his phone in his hands; it was ringing.

"Hi, Frank," he answered, exasperated and handing me my yoga pants to put on. All I was wearing was a t-shirt and my long bathrobe.

"We're coming down now," he said and hung up as I tossed my robe on the couch and finished getting dressed.

As soon as we exited the elevator, we saw Frank and Richard. The police had two men in custody: the doorman Frank didn't trust and one of the men who delivered the furniture for the media room.

"You little son of a bitch," I heard Frank say through clenched teeth. "Your grandfather won't save you this time." He and Richard walked over to us when they realized we were standing there.

"Caught them hacking this hard drive up to the building's main server. Any electrical device that has Wi-Fi capabilities and can play a video would be seeing the contents of what's on there. They said someone paid them big money to do it," Richard explained.

"The police have all their information as well. In the mean time, Richard found something on his own," Frank said, handing us a manila envelope. I opened it and pulled out a sequence of pictures taken of Lena in some bodega. She was ripping open a prepaid cell phone package. She looked like she was texting from one phone to the other. Then the pics showed her going into a store, coming out and tossing the phone in the garbage. When the PI retrieved the phone out of the trashcan, it was Nathan's phone number with *the* picture sent from it.

"What was on the hard drive?" I already knew in the back of my mind what was on it, but I had to ask anyway.

Frank simply nodded and said that we were definitely *not* in the clouds any longer, but he thinks we're safe.

"I'll destroy it." Nathan held out his hands for the hard drive.

"I will. I want to make sure there are no duplicates floating around before I erase it, wipe it useless with a high-powered magnet and melt it down to nothing," Richard assured us.

"Thanks, man." Nathan shook his hand.

*I hope there's no more floating around out there. Bad enough the world has one of my ass bent over, wearing next to nothing.*

"Frank, thank you. Thank you for putting Nathan before everything. I don't know what I'd do without you." I reached up and hugged him.

"Well, you better figure it out soon because I'm going on a five-week cruise with Annie next month." He smiled.

"Holy shit, really? Frank. Oh my god, I'm so happy for you," I squealed.

"Well, Nathan and I have been chatting a lot about him taking some time off from on-screen and maybe doing some more work behind the scenes. Hence the media mancave upstairs." He nodded behind him.

"Yeah, he mentioned something about taking some time off," I said with a smile.

"He'd do anything for you, you know that?" He kissed my forehead.

"I know. I'm pretty effin' lucky," I gushed.

"He's pretty effin' lucky too." Frank put his fist up and I laughed.

"Please don't make it go boom," I teased.

"Ohhhh, good one. Ya lucky punk." He laughed and we bumped knuckles.

# chapter eighteen

"BABE?" I CALLED OUT to Nathan and dropped my bags on the kitchen table. "Nathan?" I called out again when I heard him talking as I walked down the hallway.

"Sure thing, Naomi. I look forward to it. Me too. Very excited. I'll send it over ASAP." He paused when he saw me, leaned close, and gave me a quick kiss. "All right. Talk soon."

He put his obnoxious wireless operator-looking headset on the table and swooped in on me for a real kiss.

"Is that a roll of quarters in your pocket, or are you just happy to see me?" I joked.

"I am always happy to see you."

Nathan took my hand and slipped it in the waistline of his pants.

He looked yummy, too, with faded jeans hanging off him in just the right way, with a hole in the knee and another by the zipper. I think I probably wore that particular hole there because, anytime he put those jeans on, I rubbed up against him like a horny cat.

"Fifteen minutes until my mom gets here." He bit my neck and then sucked on the same spot.

"Stop. We can't now. Your mom will be here any second." I laughed and swatted at him before I turned and picked up a piece of mail sitting on the counter. It was from the DNA lab.

"Heh, took them long enough I totally forgot about this. Rachel and I did these DNA tests we saw advertised on the Maury Povich show." I held up the envelope.

Nathan looked at me funny. "Were you afraid *you are not the mother*?" He laughed at his own joke.

"No, oh my God, you're so stupid." I laughed with him. "These are genealogy DNA tests. They can tell you your heritage and trace your family's roots. We thought it was pretty cool. So we did it." I opened and read it.

"Looks like I'm eighty-two percent Italian, ten percent Caucasian and eight percent Irish, and I have five living blood relatives according to vital statistics. Damn, I'm a mutt." I stuck my lower lip out in a pout.

"Baby, I'll take your mutt butt any day over a purebred." He grabbed my ass and then smacked it.

"That's right. I know you will," I teased.

The elevator dinged and we separated again.

"You're mom's early." I walked to the door and opened it before she could knock.

"Where's my boy?" I asked, but it wasn't Fiona. It was Rachel and she looked rough.

"Hey, what's up?" I pulled her inside.

"Can I hang out for a little bit?" Rachel asked, but her shoes were already off and she was halfway down for the count on my couch.

"Rachel, have you been…drinking?" I asked her. I'm sure I sounded confused because I *was* confused.

"Rachel, you stink like a bowery bum."

"Yep. I've added daytime drunk to my résumé. Check." She slurred face-down on my couch.

"Okay, why?" I sat and moved her hair off her face when she turned her head, so she could breathe better.

"Why not?" She threw one arm up, then dropped it to the floor and laughed.

*Oh, man. She's really lit.*

"Well, I'm going to make some phone calls," Nathan said, backing out slowly.

"No, no, I want you to stay for this and hear me," Rachel announced.

She attempted to hold herself up and speak, but only one of those things was happening, so she decided to speak. I guessed it didn't take as much strength.

"I got a letter from the DNA testing place. Remember when we did that?" Rachel slurred and sat up, pointing sloppily at me. Then she blew the curls out of her face.

"Yep, I got it right in there." She gave me a thumbs up, then let her hand drop with a thud on her lap.

"Rachel, what the hell is it you're trying to tell us?" I tried so hard to hide my laugh but she knew me... Even drunk, she knew me.

"Don't laugh at me, bitch. Go look at the letter. In my bag. Hey, you, hot guy that gives up a multi-million-dollar career for this sack of tits here..." At that point, Rachel pulled a Diana Ross-Lil' Kim moment and pretty much felt me up. "But what nice ones they are." She snorted. "You have impeccable taste, by the way. Fetch me my bag, please."

Rachel held her arm up as if she was giving a royal command, and then it swung down to her lap.

Nathan just shook his head and gave a quick laugh while he handed over her bag.

"Yank thooo. I mean... Thank you," she said.

"I'm calling Tyler to come get her," Nathan mumbled to me.

"You do that. Please do. He won't come and get me. He isn't going to want all these damaged goods." Rachel ran her hand up her neck, to her head and back down.

"Read the damn letter," she snapped at me.

"Fine." I fished it out of her purse and opened it up.

"Out loud. Like that Twilight kid said, 'Say it. Out loud.'"

She busted out in an uncontrollable laugh and then stopped. "Okay, read it now."

*Christ, she's tanked.*

"Dear Ms. Fallon,

Your test results conclude that you are sixty-two percent Samoan and thirty-eight percent Columbian. Attached you will find the names of all recorded living relatives per vital statistics..." My voice trailed off. It listed her father and a sister amongst them.

*Da fuq?*

"Rachel, not only is your father alive but you have a sister? That's amazing. Are you going to call and find out?" I handed her back the paper.

"A fucking father," she slurred out.

"He didn't want me when I was a kid, but I bet you that ugly-ass vase over there he'll want me now that I'm all grown up and he doesn't have to pay child support." Rachel slumped over on her side again on the couch.

"Well, first of all, I'm not betting you something I already own. And if it's so ugly, why would you want to bet it? If you win, you win the ugly vase." I tried to get her mind off the problem at hand.

"Don't try your double-talk hocus pocus with me, bitch. And I want to win it so I can smash it." She hiccupped and then laughed.

I couldn't help it; I laughed too.

Nathan came back out and announced that Tyler was on his way. It seemed she'd been gone since five in the morning or maybe longer. Five was when Tyler got up and realized she was gone.

"Four," Rachel shouted, and then I think she passed out.

Nathan just stared at me with a look of uncertainty.

"What?" I asked.

"Four a.m.? Or is she dreaming of teeing off at the ninth hole?" He chuckled.

"Look at her. Who the hell knows?" I shook my head.

Tyler came to collect Rachel and bring her home. He'd been worried sick about her all day. When I asked him why he didn't call me to see if she was here, he told me he'd tried but I didn't answer.

"Ugh, sorry. I get shoddy service up here on cloudy days."

Tyler scooped her up and carried her down and, with Nathan's help, got her in the car. We said goodbye to Tyler.

"Call me later, dude. Let me know how she's doing." Nathan gave him a halfassed brohug.

Meanwhile, Fiona was getting out of a different car.

"Well, look who's fashionably late," I teased her. She was dressed to the nines.

"Hot date tonight, eh?" I asked. "Spin around, let me see the back of that dress."

Fiona handed the baby to me and then spun around slowly.

"Snazzy, lady. Ready to pound that concrete jungle. Where ya headed?"

"We're taking swing lessons over at Copello's." She absolutely beamed.

"Oh, really? Swing lessons, you say. Well, have fun and be careful."

I gave her a kiss and Nathan gave her a quick hug and a big smile. I loved it when he smiled so brightly his eyes shined.

"Look at your daddy. Look at him. You are going to be quite the heartbreaker when you grow up, kid," I said to Nate, and Nathan leaned over and kissed me.

"All right, you two, enough already. Let me kiss my girl goodbye." Fiona leaned over and kissed my forehead.

"And now my favorite boy," she said, and when Nathan leaned over, she bent and kissed the baby.

I tried to hold back a laugh but a little one squeaked by.

"Ma? What the hell?" Nathan complained with a laugh.

"What? You had to know you got demoted back to the kid's table when this one came home," she teased him.

"Goodbye, Mom. Don't kill Dad swingin'," he teased her and she smacked his arm.

"Why do you have to be so mouthy? I'm your mother," she teased him back. "Now give me a kiss and be a good boy."

"Bye, Ma, have fun," I said as I took Nate's hand and had him wave goodbye too. She blew him kisses as the car pulled away.

"So, your parents are swingers?" I busted out laughing.

"Yeah, right. Imagine that. My mother would shank a bitch if they went near my father," he joked.

"I think it's amazing how they're still so in love after all these years." I bounced Nate up and down.

The kids were out like lights by eight, so Nathan and I shared a long, hot, relaxing bath. By nine fifteen, Nathan was out cold as well.

I sat on the chaise and stared out at the city while I mindlessly rubbed lotion on my legs. I took off my robe and slipped a shirt and panties on.

I wiped my hands of the excess lotion and got in bed. I watched Nathan sleep for a minute until I realized I was doing it and decided it was way creepy.

I picked up Nathan's journal and opened it. We'd read past Halloween already, so things couldn't be too bad after that. I could read it without him.

*December 6th*

I am happy to report that Edna's husband Master Sergeant Dominick Cucuzzo is warm in his own bed just in time for Christmas.

Also, I overheard Mom asking Tyler if he would mind picking up the kid's Christmas presents, find out what size boots the mamma wears, and if Rachel would mind wrapping them up as a favor for her. I'm past confusion... I'm on a mission. Oh, and I shaved the beard. It was time. RIP beard.

*December 10th*

It's 3 a.m. This is the third night I've woken up in a panic from the same dream. It's her...calling my name, over and over. I have my arms around her, but she's trying to get away from me. The blood is from her lip, but I can't see her face... I hurt her? Is this what everyone is trying to hide from me? I'm a woman-beating monster. Is this what *they don't want me to know? If this is true, I'm a coward and I don't deserve to be protected from the truth.*

I looked ahead after the last entry I read to see how much remained. There was only one more entry left, so I decided I wanted him to read it with me.

"Babe, wake up." I nudged him.

He mumbled a bit and wrapped his arm around me. I knew what would wake him up. I took his hand and slid it down my shorts and under my panties. The man had a knack for knowing what was in his hand and how to work it. Right away, I could feel him stir and I pressed his hand against me harder. That was all it took. He took his free hand, grabbed under my kneecap and yanked me down so we were face to face.

"You needed something?" He worked his fingers a little faster with a little bit more pressure.

"Uh huh," I moaned as I kissed him.

"What do you need?" Nathan stopped, rubbed up and down, and then in. Rinse, repeat, I was a mess.

"I wanted you to read your last entry with me." I grabbed his shoulder and bit down, just how he liked it.

"Did you say entry? If you insist, ma'am." He rolled onto his back, taking me with him so I was on top.

"Say it again," he said, grabbing my hips and sliding me across him.

The material between us was getting wetter and wetter. He knew what he was doing to me and he loved it.

"Entry." I leaned down and kissed him, then laughed.

"Good girl." He slid his hands under my shirt, took one breast in each hand and tugged.

"Oh, god."

I reacted the only way I knew how when he pulled that slow and steady rubbin' and tuggin' shit. I came apart and he immediately had his hand between my legs to feel it. He loved to feel what he did to me, and that was when Nathan lost control.

He lifted me off him, guided my head down and pulled me up by my hips to get behind me. He tore my panties off and took no mercy on me as he lined himself up and pushed into me. He wrecks me every time. I swear the man took multiple-orgasm classes. He and I knew what each other wanted, when we wanted it, and how we wanted it—and amazingly, it was never a repeat episode. It was always something new each time, yet familiar and safe. I truly believe a higher power created Nathan and me for one another. He's my perfect match.

I could feel it building again as he went deeper and deeper with each thrust. When he touched me, I was done again. He wrapped his hand around the front of me and played me until my entire body twitched; it was one continuous wave after another.

Then he suddenly stopped and got off the bed.

"Stand up and wrap your legs around me," Nathan commanded me.

*Yes, sir.* "With pleasure."

I slipped around him. He kissed me and sucked on me until we reached the window. He brought us down to the ground with his back to the window, me on top.

"Keep your eyes open the whole time, understand? Watch the city go by. I want to see everything in your face. Don't hold back." He bit down on my neck and took my breast in his hand as his guided himself in with the other.

I didn't make it thirty seconds before he had me where he wanted me again. I closed my eyes and he grabbed my hips hard, moving me back and forth.

"Open them. Look at me."

*Fuck.* That's all it took. I'd come undone again, and I could feel it was almost his time, so I picked up the pace and the pressure. Ten seconds later, he was mine all over again.

# chapter
## *nineteen*

December 13th

Tonight was the night. I had every intention of getting the truth out of Tyler tonight. It was a weekend, so the bar closed late. I knew he'd be there to wait for Rachel. Every weekend I've watched him get there between 10 and 11 p.m. They leave about 3 a.m.

I was done allowing them to shelter me from whatever wrong I did. I probably deserved to get shot. I blanked it out for a reason.

I saw the bouncer bring something over to the building. The kid answered.

Jesus Christ, I've turned into a stalker. Edna came down tonight to bring me some hot chocolate and tell me the good news. Her Dominick was home. Of course, I already knew that.

She told me that a Secret Santa had volunteered

**120**

to pay for all his medical needs at home with a live-in nurse for as long as he needs it, along with basic housing expenses. She handed me the hot chocolate and gave my other hand a squeeze. When she said, "God bless whoever opened their heart like this to us." I couldn't help but get all choked up from the tears in her eyes.

She told me she had to get back inside—it was cold, and she and Dominick liked to watch reruns of *Murder She Wrote* together. Before she went inside, she patted my cheek and said, "You're a good boy; I can see it in your eyes and ya know, Nate, I never noticed that without that beard you could be in the movies... I bet you'd be the next James Dean."

I laughed, and suddenly I didn't feel like a bad guy... I knew I couldn't have hurt any woman. I felt odd... what was that feeling? Happiness? But, even more so, another emotion took the wheel and nailed the gas pedal. I was doing Mach 5 straight into a feeling that overwhelmed me... It was love. I LOVED someone just like that. Edna was me. Metaphorically, of course...but I loved someone like she loved her Dominick. Real, raw and everlasting. I just had to find her. And something real told me she was behind that door across the street.

As I approached the building, I could hear "It's the Most Wonderful Time of the Year" playing from the roof. I stared at the steps for a minute, then I took in a deep breath, walked up the stoop and pressed the buzzer. After about 30 seconds, I went to ring it again and my heart stopped.

I heard a kid's voice ask, "Who is it?" I said I was sorry, but then I asked if I knew who lived in the building. I saw the curtain move upstairs. After another few seconds, I heard muffled shouting coming from up there as well. I began to doubt my decision to face this head-on. Then I heard it... The voice... Her voice... It was a bit shaky, but I'd know that voice anywhere.

"Go away," was all she said. I told her I had an accident a few months back and I don't remember much, but I know that this place is like a magnet that draws me in. I told her that she didn't need to be afraid—that I'm not dangerous or anything like that—but that I just couldn't stay away.

Holy shit, had I sounded desperate and scary?

When she finally replied, she sounded like she was about to cry. All I heard was, "You don't know who lives here, Nathan. Now please go away."

That was it. NATHAN. Nobody called me Nathan except her...well, the voice who I now know is her. The rest of the world calls me Nate.

"Oh," was my grand response. IDIOT. OH? My god, I was the world's biggest pussy.

I needed to pull my shit together quick. I stayed there for a few minutes, just looking around, trying to figure out my next move. When I couldn't come up with anything that wouldn't end with a restraining order against me, I walked away.

I got about three buildings down when I heard someone curse. I jogged back to her stoop. I waited for her to turn around, but she didn't. I started towards her, asking her if she was the woman I'd just spoken with. When I got within about three feet of her, I had no control. Auto-pilot took over and I was pretty sure I was going to crash and burn after this one, but I didn't give a fuck. I somehow knew she was everything to me, and I didn't even know who she was. I had to keep talking or I was going to lose it. I was behind her by that point, and when I got a whiff of her hair, a shower came to mind. I know. Fucking weird, right?

I told her that I didn't mean to upset her—that I was

just at a loss in my life right now and felt so empty and alone. That I couldn't understand for the life of me why this building comforted me so much.

Hey, it was better than "I stalk this building to stay sane," ok? I didn't know what to do, because she was quiet again, but I could hear her sniffle, and then I saw her shoulders move. She was crying. Holy good Christ...going there was a bad idea. I saw her take in a deep breath and she asked me to "just go." I inched forward so I was nearly touching her. She smelled like home. I knew this was the one. I had to know what I did to make her so upset that she couldn't even look at me. She turned around and looked up at me. I had no words. Her eyes locked with mine. Gorgeous green eyes—eyes that sucked the air right out of me. All I could do was tell her how beautiful she was.

What she said next threw me off. She disagreed with me, saying she wasn't a "skinny blonde skank" as she stared at her belly. I tried to explain that I was just trying to find myself. She came back at me with something about finding more than just myself. My expression must have affected her, because her face turned bright red and she looked like she was going to punch me—but then, boom went the dynamite, because she exploded. She laid into me about all the women I had been with over the last 6 months, "all the sex," and even used the terms "sexcapades" and "Sexual Olympics."

That broke me... I cracked a smile and—at first—she did too, but then she was all serious again. When she was finally finished, I said I wasn't quite sure why I was discussing my sex life with her, but I felt like I was supposed to, so I told her that I don't remember the last time I had sex—literally. She didn't believe me.

Wow, this firecracker had quite the mouth on her. I loved it.

Then Tyler showed up, calling my name and dragging me off for a beer next door. When we got inside the bar, it was still packed, but they were winding down. Apparently I wasn't popular with anyone who worked there...especially the big guy over in the corner. He was definitely trying to shrink my head with his mind. No doubt about it. I saw Rachel answer her phone and then glare over at me... She wanted to blow my head up, not shrink it.

We sat and waited for them to close up, clean up, and get out of there. It was nearly 3 a.m. Everyone was gone—it was just Tyler, Rachel, and me left in the quiet bar.

Rachel tossed her stuff on the counter in a huff and stood quietly, giving me her all-familiar dirty look. I knew this couldn't be good. I told Rachel I don't know what it is I did exactly...and that's when it happened. She exploded. Hands flailing, screaming curses, she grabbed her phone and started playing some boy band song. She jumped on the bar and started dancing. I thought she'd truly lost her mind. Then she rambled on about Jordie, Emma, and a baby. How a crazy-ass terrorist who was actually Jordie's presumed dead husband had actually flipped on our country and then attacked me.

I mean, words were flying everywhere and they made no sense. I pushed off the bar and headed outside. I needed to breathe. I needed air. Jordie? Jordie... Jordie.

I'd just gotten to the street when BAM, flash after flash went off in my mind. It was all back. Every single detail. Every single memory. I held my head where I was hit. I ran over to her building. JORDAN MARIE SPAGNATO. Emma... Emma was the kid... And the baby—our baby. HOLY FUCKING SHIT. It was all there.

I ran back into the bar and yanked Rachel into my arms. I just started screaming, "Thank you, holy shit, thank you!" I swear I almost broke her... She is so tiny and I was swinging her around like a rag doll. Tyler stopped me and saved Rachel. He was smiling. They both were. I remembered!

I needed to get over there. I needed to...but then I had a better idea.

Rachel had wanted to tell me something all along. She laughed and told me that she was just trying to shrink that big-ass head of mine. I started laughing. I asked if she could let me in so I could get to the rooftop. I'd wait for Jordie there. Thankfully, she agreed.

Rachel let me up. I saw the wireless speakers sitting on the table, so I synced my phone with it, searched for the song and played it. A few minutes later, I heard the door open. I turned and there she was: messy hair, sleepy eyes, and angry as hell from the looks of it. She could have had a Saint Bernard on her head and she still would have been the most beautiful woman I had ever laid eyes on. There she was. My Jordie.

That's really about it. I don't have the time to go through the rest because I just heard Emma wake up. I want to go downstairs and surprise her. I won't wake Jordan.

That's how I ended up finally Finding Nathan.

I closed up his journal and placed it on my nightstand.

"And here we are." I smiled.

"Here we are." He gave a quick laugh.

"You beat my vag up, you know; it's off limits for at least two days," I scolded him playfully.

"Oh, no. I can kiss it and make it better," he offered.

"Just kiss me." I leaned in.

"Anytime, anyplace, sweetheart," my Nathan obliged sweetly.

His phone was buzzing but he ignored it. After a few minutes, it buzzed again, but he still paid it no mind.

When we woke in the morning, it was still going off, so he finally checked it.

"Babe, it's Tyler. Have you heard from Rachel?" Nathan asked, sitting up and patting me on the leg to wake me thoroughly.

"No, why? Not since we threw her in the drunk tank," I joked, stifling a yawn.

When he didn't respond but kept reading the texts, I knew something was up.

"What's wrong?" I panicked and grabbed my phone off my nightstand. There were no new calls or texts.

"I got nothing. You?"

"I just texted and asked him where he was so I can meet up with him and help," Nathan answered.

"Help with what, Nathan?" My voice was borderline hysterical.

His phone went off again and he read the text. His face was expressionless.

"What does it say? Nathan? Is she okay?" I fired off the questions in rapid-fire succession as my panic increased.

He read the text aloud to me. "Thanks, dude, but I have to go find her and bring her back."

As he typed his response, he spoke it aloud. "What are you going to do? Are you sure I can't come help?"

Nathan's phone buzzed again.

Tyler: No, really. Thanks, man. Nobody can help when it comes to finding Rachel...

# Finding Rachel Excerpt

My friendship with Jordie was the closest I'd ever come to believing that some things were meant to be. For whatever reason…we just clicked. She was one of the only people I could call a "fugly slut" and she'd respond with something along the lines of, "That's better than being a dirty-ass stank ho." I knew we'd be friends forever.

Fast forward past a whole lotta fucked up shit, and enter Tyler Duncan, the love of my life and the only man who never ran out on me. I didn't give him the chance because I bailed first.

Now, Jordie—I knew that bitch would be a little harder to get rid of. She's relentless; even the shit I said to her before I left didn't stop her from searching for me. I'll never forget the look on her face before I walked out her door. I still have to hold my stomach so my insides don't fall out through my ass, because I feel so sick.

*"Jordan, I don't see what the problem is. It's not like I exist in your world anymore…except to serve as your bar wench. I'm done, I quit. I quit the bar, I quit Tyler, and I definitely quit you. You're all happy hunky-dory shacked up with your mooooovie star husband and your perrrfect life. Why the fuck would you even want me around anymore?" I yelled at Jordie, biting back the tears as I balled my fists, ready to beat myself over the head with them.*

*"Rachel, I love you, you're my best—"*

*"Yeah, yeah, I know. I'm your best friend, right?" I interrupted her. "But that's just it. I'm not anymore. He is. Nathan is. Him, your kids, they are everything. And I get it, that's cool, I'm fucking ecstatic over the goddamned moon for you…so just let me go without all this bull shit, Jordan." I turned my back to her and faced the door because I couldn't hold back the tears anymore.*

"Tyler loves you, Rachel. He's been up for days looking for you. He hasn't slept, he hasn't eaten, and he hasn't stopped searching the streets for you. He's worried sick and heartbroken. He can't even help you because he doesn't know what's wrong. Fuck, I don't even know what's wrong, Rach. Talk to me," she demanded.

With my back still turned to her, I sniffled and stared at the door. "I contacted my father. I spoke with him." I turned back around to face her even though my face was leaking like a mofo by then.

"And?" Jordie asked impatiently.

"And? Well, long story short, it turns out he didn't really abandon us and I have a sister. Not a half sister...a full-blooded sister." I waited for Jordan to close her mouth and put her eyes back in their sockets as she sat down on the couch. "My mother... She told him to go and to take my three-year-old sister with him. He wanted to take me too, but she said no, that she was keeping me. He knew why, too...because she knew he'd pay child support for me. I was her meal ticket. As he told me, I didn't believe it, until he sent me an email. It was a scan of a handwritten letter from my mom, telling him I was killed in a bus accident. That he needed to send money for a cremation because I was too badly mangled for an open-casket funeral and that she'd send him some ashes. I was fifteen at the time she wrote it, Jordie. There was also a picture included of him and my sister sitting in the garden they made in my memory. Even had a plaque that said, In Memory of a beautiful daughter, sister and soul, our Rachel. How about that shit?" I said as we both sobbed like two little bitches.

"Rach...if you want to go meet them, I'll go with you. I'll call Nathan and make him come home right now, and I'll pack my shit. You and me, let's go. You can set things straight and maybe have a relationship with them. Then come home and get back to being the old Rachel, because I miss my best friend. I can't stand to see you in so much pain all the time," she pleaded.

I knew she was right. I needed to go see the life I missed out on because my mother was an evil succubus who thrived on others' misery. I also needed to do it alone. After this cluster fuck, it'd only be a matter of time before Tyler bailed on me. Who would blame him? My life went from stable and happy to 'Houston, we have a problem' in four-point-two seconds.

*"How can I marry him if I don't even know who I am anymore?" I said, and adjusted my purse over my shoulder. "You've got what you need, Jordan, and it's not me anymore. It was a good run, biotch. I love you, but I've got to get out of here. Start over."*

*I walked over to her and we hugged.*

*"Rachel, please stay. No, fuck that, I won't let you leave. We're sisters. I love you."*

*Jordie was in a full-blown ugly cry and she hugged me tighter. She wouldn't let me go.*

*I had to shove her off me. Fuck, what came next would hurt the both of us for a very long time...but I had to, or she would never have let me go. This was worse than breaking up with Tyler. I mean, if I had actually broken it off with Tyler face-to-face, instead of me running off like a fucking coward.*

*"God dammit, Jordan, why can't you just do one fucking thing that I ask you? You're so effin' spoiled it makes me sick. Just forget you ever knew me, you selfish bitch, because after I walk out that door I'm done. You're no longer in my life, in my thoughts, or in my heart. I won't miss you, I won't think about you. I'm finally going to get my life together instead of always putting yours back together." I hissed out at her, turned, and walked out the door.*

"Rachel? Rachel? Stop being a space cadet and take this to table eight. *Please*," Kyla said to me as she handed me two Piña Coladas.

"Table eight, coming right up." I rolled my eyes when I turned to walk off.

*Bitch. Who the fuck even says "space cadet" anymore?* Kyla does, that's who.

Kyla was my floor manager at Rain Night Club at The Palms Casino in Las Vegas. She was nice enough to work under, it's just that I wasn't accustomed to being told what to do. I usually called the shots. A lot had changed in the last two and a half months. I didn't have to think about what I left behind until they found me. Damn Nathan and Frank, with their money and mad detective skills. I was hoping to just leave quietly, and Tyler would accept the fact that I got cold feet and wasn't the marrying type.

# acknowledgements

To you, yeah you, the person reading this, thank you for being here. It means more than you

Jenni and Patti, the two of you are my sane side. LOL You guys keep me in check and I love you

Jess, I hate that we live a million miles apart. My bestie. I miss youuuu.

Heidi McLaughlin, just because you're still awesome and you get me.

Murphy Rae thank you for helping me make this book kick ass. No matter how awkward I am.

Sommer Stein, once again you've created a masterpiece other's call a cover.

Travis, because you can take Heidi's hockey trash talk like the man you are. I love you.

And one last thing…Unicorns for Life. Yo.